GIRL IN BED THREE

SARAH SHERIDAN

Print ISBN 978-1-914614-71-2

ALSO BY SARAH SHERIDAN

For Nicole, here's to many more cups of coffee.

CHAPTER ONE

'I come from the perfect family,' I said. My words were slower than usual – I felt ill with tiredness. My eyelids ached; it was a hard fight not to give in to sleep. I knew the detectives in front of me were here to help, it was important that I talk to them. We all needed answers. It was still less than twenty-four hours since the unspeakable destruction happened that smashed my parents, siblings and I apart. I sighed.

The detective sitting at the end of my hospital bed nodded and waited. A minute ago, she'd asked me to describe my home life, but I was still struggling to find the right words, any words, to even begin an answer with. How was it possible to define the bizarre hell of my family – that for years had been masked so expertly by perfect-looking parents? Normally, if outsiders enquired, I just said everything was fine. Just one word: fine. And there *had* been questions over the years, because occasionally there'd been signs an outsider couldn't overlook – like bruises or our plummeting weight – that suggested perhaps not everything was okay in the Macreavy household. But us kids – me, Jack, Luke and Rachel – had all learnt early on that if we said anything to strangers about our family life, nothing *ever* got better for us. It actually got worse. Either we weren't taken seriously, or my parents managed to smooth our words over with their own slick lies and reassurances. And as a result of our candidness, our punishments at home would go from bad to unmanageable. So in the end we'd stopped trying to explain. Just accepted and adapted. As I tried to think, the antiseptic smell of the ward hung in the still air around me.

Right now, in the Torquay and Paignton Hospital, I couldn't make sense of life. Everything that had felt real for years – even though most of it was bad – was fragmenting and drifting off into some unknown time and space. A couple of hours ago a nice doctor had gently told me that my parents were dead. I'd felt nothing but a soothing numbness when he'd said that. No regret, no sadness or grief. But still, it signified a massive shift, a change. A fog of nothingness filled my head, and I liked it very much. I wanted it to stay, get bigger, balloon until it filled every crevice. It was so thick it blanked out any mental pain. But one question kept nagging at me: what was going to happen to me now?

'At least that's what everyone thought until last night,' I went on, swallowing, turning my empty water bottle over and over in my hands. Could I really say this – admit to the truth of our lives, my upbringing – after all these years of forced secrecy? A flash of nausea rolled through me, and the bottle slid against my now sweating palms. Come on, Sophie, you can do this – I pep-talked myself. You don't have to be scared anymore. 'Now maybe the truth about my parents will come out at last, and people will see how screwed up they really were,' I said, my words speeding up. 'They've had everyone fooled for years. We tried to explain that to so many people when we were younger, but no one believed us, so we just gave up. They've been treating us badly all this time, and no one has ever known.' There. I did it. I held my breath, half expecting the world to implode because I'd broken the family code of silence. Or that a ring of fire would come into being, and the Devil himself would drag me through to eternal damnation – one of Iris's favourite threats if she thought we were misbehaving. But nothing happened – everything in the room stayed the same.

Detective Warner blinked, nodded and continued making notes. She must have been sitting on the end of my bed for at least half an hour now; she'd already asked me if I knew of anyone who wanted to harm my family, if my parents had ever expressed any concerns about one or more people, if somebody I knew had shown signs of being violent. I watched while her black scratchy writing quickly filled up a fresh new page in her notebook. Industrious, Dad would have called her. A worker bee. A constant 'doer'; someone who was always busy. Dad always had a label for people, like he needed them to fit neatly into his predetermined categories. I never really understood why, because in my experience people are too complex for that. Too messy, with hundreds of overlapping traits and inconsistencies. But labelling people made Dad happy, so that's what he did. I was 'difficult', Rachel was 'pathetic', Luke was 'sullen' and Jack was 'a problem' – at least, according to Dad. It was the least harmful of his habits.

My breaths were slowing down again now, and for some reason it struck me how young Detective Warner looked compared with the other investigator she'd arrived with – the tall, quiet man with the grey moustache standing in the corner of the room. His eyes hadn't left me since he took up his unmoving position, and I didn't like it. He was a thinker; an observer, Dad would have said. A people watcher who took in every scene. Detective Warner looked up, her biro poised over a new line.

'And you can't remember anything else that happened

3

yesterday evening, other than the details you've already told me?'

'No.' I shook my head, and repeated again what she already knew: that the last thing I recalled about the horrific events of yesterday's dark October evening was being told – ordered – to get into my dad's blue SUV. 'After that it's a blank, and the next thing I remember is waking up in hospital.'

Detective Warner nodded and scribbled some more.

'Thank you. And how old are you, Sophie?'

'Nineteen,' I said, then sighed. I knew what would be coming next.

The detective's head snapped up.

'Nineteen?' she repeated, her eyebrows raising. 'Wow, I thought you were much younger than that. I was ready for you to say fourteen; fifteen at the most.'

'Yep.' I nodded, and a twinge of pain ricocheted through my neck and left shoulder. 'That's what everyone says. My parents often withheld food from us, so we probably didn't grow as much as we should have. Especially Rachel; she's twelve but she looks about eight. How is she, by the way?' I looked from Detective Warner to her silent colleague. A pang of worry tinged with annoyance shook through me. 'I keep asking the nurses but they just say they don't know anything as she was taken to a different hospital.' I'm close to all my siblings – we've had to have each others' backs from an early age – but Rachel and I have the tightest bond. I can tell what she's thinking without her having to say anything, and she often finishes my sentences without noticing she's doing it. We've never been apart since she arrived, not even for one night, so it's really weird not being with her now. I kind of feel like one of my limbs is missing.

'Ah.' Detective Warner's eyes flashed over to meet the gaze of the man in the corner. I saw him give a small nod. 'Listen,

Sophie love, there's no easy way to tell you this, but I'm afraid Rachel didn't make it. The doctors did everything they could for her, but she was pronounced dead late this morning...'

The sick rose so fast in my throat that despite my best efforts I couldn't reach the cardboard bowl the nurse had placed on my side table in time.

'And the boys?' I managed, wiping my mouth, as tears welled up and splashed down my cheeks. I literally couldn't believe this was all happening. The detective in the corner grabbed a roll of blue tissue from a shelf and walked forward, placing it on the bed next to me, before retreating back to his original position.

Detective Warner turned towards him, and he nodded at her again.

'Well you see, Sophie,' he said, his voice steady and quiet. 'That's why we need you to try and remember as much as you can about last night. Any details, no matter how small – even if they seem insignificant to you. We need to piece together what happened, how and why your mother, father and sister were found stabbed to death in the family car on Meadcoombe Cliff. You were very lucky to escape the attack with the wounds you received – I know some of them are quite deep but they'll heal. I've got several officers looking at CCTV in the area to see if we can join up the dots and understand what led up to this terrible crime. However, the strange thing is that so far we haven't been able to locate your brothers. They weren't found in the car with the rest of you, even though the one bit of CCTV we've recovered as yet clearly shows that they definitely *were* in the car with you all at the start of the evening. An extensive search of Meadcoombe Cliff has been going on since just after one o'clock this morning – when the crime was reported by passers-by. But so far we haven't been able to find Luke or Jack anywhere...'

CHAPTER TWO

I was four when Iris and Don Macreavy adopted me. They couldn't have children of their own, they said; although they never explained why and I didn't dare ask. My earliest memory of my mum – Iris – is her telling me how she and Dad had saved me from a bad life, and that I should say thank you to them for that. I was a 'drug baby', Mum told me many times throughout my life. When I was born my biological mother was addicted to crack cocaine, and therefore so was I. Which explained my erratic behaviour, Mum often said. My natural wilfulness and disobedience, even in the face of worsening 'corrective' punishments. I don't remember much about my life before I became a Macreavy, other than one memory of my granny on my biological mum's side – Violet. I lived with her for a couple of years after social services took me away from my natural mum. But Violet didn't know how to raise a child either, apparently, so one day – when my social worker came for a visit and found me eating dirt in the garden, as skinny as a rake even though I was only three – I was taken into care. My one memory of Granny Violet is of watching her face as she stared at the TV. I don't know why I remember that, but her face was yellow – probably all the cigarettes – and had wrinkles all over it, like an old pickled walnut.

'Everyone loves Iris and Don Macreavy,' I remember our priest saying to my friend's mum once, when I was six. We were standing by one of the cake tables at the school fair at the time. And he was right – everyone loved them. The parents, the teachers, everyone at church. That was a term before Iris took me and my siblings out of state education for good, so she could 'homeschool' us. That was before the *thing* happened – the one my parents never really explained to us – that made them leave the outside church and set up one inside the house...

My parents – Iris and Don, my adoptive ones – have always been everyone's golden couple. Even after they moved away from the church. Everyone in the community seems to know of them. For a start, they looked the part – my mum had naturally good bone structure, and her face was angular and striking. She had a strong smile, white teeth, golden hair and legs up to her armpits. Any clothes she put on automatically made her look like a model. Her eyes were ice blue and deep set. Men thought they were beautiful, but I came to fear her gaze very early on. I don't look anything like her – which is not surprising really – with my short height, skinny childish body, long, lank brown hair and hazel eyes. She'd certainly been at the front of the queue when genetics were handed out, whereas clearly I was not. My dad was also super attractive. He was naturally charming, and could befriend anyone in a matter of minutes. He had brown hair that only started thinning on top last year, and he generally wore it quite long and brushed over to one side. He was tall and had a roundish face that creased up nicely when he smiled. He loved his wife – my crazy mother – to the point of obsession, and would do anything to make her happy. They looked good together, everyone said so. In the days when we all still went out together as a family and were allowed to talk to outsiders.

Mum and Dad were pillars of the community when I was young. They were both devout Catholics when they adopted me, and I have memories of watching them doing readings in church. I thought they were so important then. They donated generously to local fundraising events – I know this because there are photos on the walls in the house of them handing over cheques from Dad's successful printing business. They were first on everyone's dinner party lists, Mum told me more than once, before us kids came along. When I was allowed to go to school when I was younger, Mum was generally surrounded by other mothers in the playground. She was always popular – people were drawn towards something magnetic in her looks and character – like flies to sticky papers.

What good actors they were. How skilful of them to create this perfect façade, one that fooled everyone in our town – Torquay. When Facebook started, it was an actual gift for my mother. She was already starting to withdraw all four of us kids from public life when it really took off, so instead of dressing us nicely and showcasing us all at church and school events, she took to posting beautiful photos of us on her Facebook page. Honestly – if I didn't know better and was an outsider looking at those pictures – I would think my sister, brothers and I were leading the best, most charmed life possible. There's one of me baking wholemeal bread, with a scattering of flour on my little apron. There's one of Jack and Luke having a snowball fight in winter, big smiles on their rosy cheeks. There's a shot of Rachel painting a beautiful rainbow picture. Then there's all four of us hugging in one photo, and watching a sunset in another.

My mother's most famous photo – the one that went viral and made both her and me famous for a while – was all due to her pretence at social concern. Whenever there was a 'cause' for her to pretend to publicly care about – so she could win Brownie points from her thousands of Facebook friends – us kids were dragged into the posturing of it all. When Iris decided to join the campaign for NHS workers to have their salaries raised, we were pictured holding posters of support. When some affordable housing was going to be knocked down in Torquay, we were dragged into her campaign for that. Sometimes – although rarely – Iris even took us along to socialist events, like the big environmental one in London when the group Destruction Revolution were protesting about the state of the planet. I was fifteen at the time (and looked about eleven), and Iris had made us all colourful signs to wear round our necks. We really looked the part, and she appeared to be the world's most caring mother. My sign said 'Act Now, and Give Me a Future'. It just so happened that a well-known beautiful environmental activist, Brianna Salotto – who, at the time, I'd never actually heard of before – was standing near me at one point, with press all around her. When she saw me and my sign, she seemed quite emotional, and came over to give me a big hug. That's when the cameras began flashing, and the next day there were photos of me and Brianna in all the papers and even on TV. You can see my mum in the background looking like the perfect caring parent. I know this because Iris showed me some clippings, and told me how lucky I was to have her for a mother.

What a perfect life, right?

Wrong. What no one knew was that Iris staged all those photos. I wasn't really allowed to bake bread, I was put into position and told to smile. She told Jack and Luke exactly how to stand in the snow, they were allowed out there for less than three minutes while she took photos – not one real snowball was thrown. Rachel didn't actually paint that rainbow picture – my mother did. And if anyone looked closely at the brush Rachel is holding in that photo they will see it doesn't actually have any paint on the bristles. My mum gave her a clean one to hold. Iris always hated mess of any kind, one of the many reasons she used to stop us from playing.

Even the activist photos were faked, we were never allowed to make the signs for them, or had any idea what we were really doing. I was *so* hungry during the Destruction Revolution rally as I hadn't been fed for hours, which was probably why I looked so suitably sad in all the press photographs with Brianna. I fully believe that Iris created this perfect-looking façade because she wanted eternal approval and love from everyone, even if it wasn't actually real. She would make lots of superficial new buddies when we went on our occasional outings, and they would 'friend' her on Facebook, then tell her what an absolutely wonderful mother she was, taking her adopted kids around to these events and giving them such a good life. But none of them ever knew the actual truth about who she really was. She was a true narcissist.

Generally, after the photos were taken and Mum had achieved her idealistic snap, we would all sink back into ourselves like well-trained robots; apathetic and quiet. Making noise in our home was a big no-no. We couldn't play, or talk loudly, or go out, or attend school or even church.

Sounds unbelievable, doesn't it? Oh, if only there'd been spy cameras around the house for all those years, then the truth would be out there and people wouldn't have to rely on just my word. I wish I was lying, making this all up, but it all happened, it really did. I became emptier and emptier on the inside over each of the past years, as though my soul was dying a slow death. I had no discernible personality, I felt like a hollow void who had no identity. I was just there as a prop to please my mother on occasion, and anger her most of the rest of the time.

If I'm honest, I have to admit that things were a bit easier for me before Luke, Jack and Rachel came along and became my younger Macreavy siblings. I'm the oldest, and it was just me with Mum and Dad for two years before the other three arrived. Like me they came from an abusive home. Into another one. They are all biological siblings – Iris and Don decided to adopt the whole lot of them altogether – as social workers didn't want them split up into different households. Before they arrived, Iris and Don were strict with me, and fairly cold – except when we were out in public and they did their loving parent act – but I didn't get punished all the time like I did when the other three came to live there. In fact, because everyone else so obviously thought my parents were wonderful, I was rather proud to be part of their family. But that didn't last long. I was six when my new siblings arrived; Luke and Jack – the twins – were four, and Rachel was only two. They all had behavioural problems to start with, it was like they were feral animals. They would poo and wee all over the carpet, never go to bed, scream all the time and the boys were violent with each other and the rest of us.

I don't think Iris and Don could cope with them, really. They'd never had to deal with any of that behaviour with me, and the out-of-control craziness that Luke, Jack and Rachel brought to the house tipped Iris over the edge. Don was out at work in those days running his printing business, so Mum was home trying to raise four of us by herself. She couldn't deal with the mess and the noise that filled every hour back then, so one day, when Jack wouldn't stop screaming and hitting Luke, she snapped and punched him so hard he slammed backwards into the wall. I can remember seeing him sliding down to the floor, a shocked look on his little face. He didn't cry, he just went limp and stayed in that position for ages. And then he was quiet for the rest of the day. Maybe because that bit of violence had worked well for her, Mum started using it more often on all of us. That's when the nightmare at home *really* started.

At first, I felt left out because of the other three's crazy family closeness, but that didn't carry on for very long. Soon all four of us were bound together as patchwork siblings, forced to stick together as the viciousness at home escalated.

Right, I need to get some sleep, but I don't think that will be possible now that I know Rachel's dead, and my brothers are missing. My brain won't even let me think about them too much right now, it's overloaded. I know I'm not showing much emotion on the outside, but I simply can't. I don't know how to. And there's always a light on in the ward, even in the middle of the night. I can't believe it, the last twenty-four hours don't seem real at all. After I threw up when the detective told me about my sister, the numbness returned – thank God – and I can't actually *feel* anything about her death now. But images of her keep flashing into my head, like on an old-fashioned TV when the screen flickers. I keep seeing her, all tiny and emaciated, staring right at me. It's like she wants me to help her, but I can't do anything, I'll never be able to help her again. Poor Rachel.

The nurse is coming over with the medicine trolley, maybe she'll give me a sleeping pill if I ask. The detectives told me my new family liaison officer is coming to the hospital tomorrow and I need to have enough energy to talk to her, especially if she has some news about where Luke and Jack are. No one knows what happened yet, who the bastard was that stabbed Mum, Dad and Rachel to death. I can't remember, and Luke and Jack aren't here to say. I need to stop the horror of it all, I need to try and remember something, or I'll go mad. Madder than I already am...

CHAPTER THREE

'She's over there,' I heard a voice call. 'The girl in bed three.'
Soft footsteps came closer, and I felt someone sit down on the end of my bed.

'Sophie?'

My eyes opened and for a minute I struggled to remember where I was. A sharp pain shot through my head as I remembered I was in hospital, and the reason for that. A pretty lady was sitting by my feet looking at me. Freaky, who on earth was this? She was wearing blue trousers and a pink top, and couldn't be more than twenty-six or seven – although I'm not very good at judging people's ages. Was she an off-duty doctor?

'Yes?'

'Hi, it's so nice to meet you,' the lady said with a warm smile. 'Sorry if I gave you a shock, I didn't mean to. I've only just arrived. I'm Lisa Denton, I'm your family liaison officer and I'll be supporting and helping you through all this, for as long as you need me to.'

'Er, hi.' I shifted myself into a sitting position. 'Thanks for coming to see me.' Weird, I thought police officers all had to wear uniform, but obviously not. The soothing smell of fresh toast filled my nostrils, and I saw a health care assistant pushing the breakfast trolley through the ward.

'No problem at all,' Officer Denton said. 'And I just wanted to say how sorry I am to hear about what's happened to your family. This must all be so hard for you.' Her big brown eyes looked genuinely pained.

I looked down at the white hospital sheet. It felt smooth beneath my hands. I clutched it. Hard was an understatement. But I still felt numb, which was weird. And good. I knew that everything that had happened was horrendous, awful, a complete and utter tragedy, but it was like my body's defence system had kicked in and stopped me from feeling the actual grief of it all. The mental images of Rachel were bad enough – she'd come to me in my dreams last night, she'd seemed so real. I'd reached out and given her a tight hug, and she'd squeezed me back. Then she'd done something strange; she'd shaken her head at me very slowly, a serious look on her face. I'd asked her what she meant, but she'd just smiled and disappeared. And I was still worrying about what was going to happen to me. Right now, the Macreavy family home was the last place I wanted to go, it would be like revisiting hell. But what else was I supposed to do? I was a naïve nineteen-year-old who looked fourteen, who had zero life experience because I'd been kept prisoner in that bloody house for so many years. Hospital seemed like the best option at the moment, but I couldn't stay here forever, could I?

I looked up.

'Officer Denton,' I said. 'Is there any news about Luke or Jack? The detective said no one's found them yet.' My brave brothers, always looking out for me and Rachel, trying their best to shield us from punishments that neither they – nor anyone else – could stop from happening. Only two years younger than me, but in some ways – because of the things they'd been through at home – they seemed old before their time. Wise and reassuring. But recently they'd seemed increasingly restless. Which hadn't surprised me; it's one thing controlling children, but teens who are turning into adults are completely different, as my parents had been finding out.

'I'm glad you asked,' Officer Denton said. 'And please, call me Lisa. Your brothers haven't been found yet, but I do have some news for you. As my colleagues Detective Pierce and Detective Warner told you yesterday, continuous searches have been conducted for both boys since your mother, father and sister were found deceased in the car on top of Meadcoombe Cliff in the early hours of Monday. I believe you've already been asked about whether you know if anyone intended harm to your family? About whether even Jack or Luke had expressed a desire to kill or maim your parents? I'm not sure if you know this, Sophie, but we've found out that Jack was assessed by a psychiatrist a few years ago, after your parents called for help when your brother caused significant damage to their house and car after an argument. In the resulting report, the psychiatrist identifies high levels of aggression in Jack, and queries a potential diagnosis of antisocial personality disorder, due to the reckless nature of his behaviour. This is obviously a cause for concern for us, as Jack has proven to be violent in the past.'

'So is he your main suspect at the moment?' I said. It was so weird to be talking about my seventeen-year-old brother like this.

'More of a person of interest,' Lisa said. 'Until we know more, we can't say anything for certain, but his past behaviour certainly means we need to find and speak with him.'

I nodded. The thing was, Jack did have an anger problem; but it was only natural really – his hostility towards Iris and Don – given how they treated us. I remembered the day when he'd vandalised the house and car, and to be honest it wasn't his fault. Iris had been in an awful mood and taken it out on him;

15

nothing he'd done had been right or good enough that day; she'd withheld all his meals, beaten him, berated him, told him he was possessed by a demon and repeatedly stated what a worthless nobody he was. He'd snapped, and taken his frustration and rage out by smashing up the living room, then keying Dad's car. So, ironically my parents had called the police, even though we could never do that when they mistreated us. But I didn't think he would actually hurt our parents; if he'd wanted to he would have done it that evening. But instead, he'd taken his rage out on inanimate objects. Jack was really nice and a good guy at heart, although no one outside his siblings knew him well enough to understand that. If he ever saw me upset, he would take the time to say kind words if he could, or check on me later to see if I was feeling better. The thing about him was that he was too intelligent to just take Iris and Don's behaviour lying down, without questioning it. He was only two years younger than me, he was too old to quietly take their pointless punishments and misused religious threats. Not that he'd ever really taken them quietly. I always loved how feisty he was, that they hadn't fully squashed his spirit. I couldn't say for sure that my brother wouldn't go as far as to kill my parents, but I knew he loved our little sister Rachel, and that he would never do anything to hurt her. So the thought of him slaying those three in the car was just too much. I didn't believe it.

'And if I'm right, yesterday you also told my colleagues about a problem your mother and father had with other church members years ago?'

I nodded again. I didn't know much about whatever trouble had happened with Iris, Don and their church, but it had been significant enough for them to leave. I'd been sad when we'd stopped going, as I'd made friends at Sunday school. I'd felt a bit more normal back then. It seemed very unlikely that a group of

Christians would do them harm though, surely? Wouldn't that be against all their most fundamental beliefs?

I thought for a minute, a dazed sensation coming over me.

'Um, hang on, what day is it today?' I said. Had I slept through the whole night? Was it morning now? I couldn't tell.

'It's Tuesday morning,' Lisa said, her voice kind. She looked down at her watch. 'Nine forty-seven, to be exact. You must be feeling very disorientated, bless you. So much has happened in a short space of time, and you're probably still in shock, Sophie. Things will seem better and easier in time, but don't put any pressure on yourself right now. That's why I'm here, to look after you and to give you as much information as I can.'

I looked at her and nodded. She was being so nice to me, her kindness felt like soothing balm on my insides. It also made me want to cry.

'Thank you,' I said. I tried to smile but my lips wouldn't bend upwards, they were stuck in a rigid line.

Lisa nodded and her eyes crinkled. Her shoulder-length brown hair fell forward a bit and she reached up to tuck it back behind her ears.

'So yesterday, there was no sign of your brothers anywhere,' she went on. 'And as your father's phone was not found in or near the car we've continued to try and track it in case the boys have it with them. Up until now there has been no signal coming from it. But I had a call from Detective Pierce early this morning, and he said a signal from your father's phone has been detected up near Compington Mount, so a team has been dispatched to investigate the area. I'll be kept informed of any developments, and of course, I'll pass any news straight on to you.'

I realised my mouth was now hanging open a bit. Compington Mount? That was miles away from both Meadcoombe Cliff and our house. Why would Dad's phone be up there, when he was found dead in the car? Could one of the boys really have it? The Mount – basically a steep hill that overlooked Torquay, was a wilderness that I was unfamiliar with. While me and my brothers and sister were rarely allowed out, one thing we did have at home were hundreds of books, with both our parents being avid readers. So that's how I'd experienced the world up to now; second-hand – through the descriptions of others. I'd devoured most of them many times over, loved the works of Charles Dickens, the Brontës and Thomas Hardy. Jane Austen was all right, but her characters were generally too happy, they lived in too much of an easy, social whirl. I preferred characters that suffered, because they made me feel better; I found their pain soothing: Amy Dorrit, Smike, and Jane Eyre – now those were my kind of people.

We also had several history and guide books about Torquay and the surrounding areas, and I'd pored over the maps in them for ages, tracing the roads and shoreline with my fingers, wondering if I'd ever have the freedom to wander round those places by myself. The books had photos too, and I'd spent a long time staring at the sea views and sandy beaches, at the pretty town with its rows of houses and church spires, the harbour – always packed with boats, at images of Compington Mount and other landmarks, soaking in everything from the books that I was hardly ever allowed to see in real life. I learnt about other towns, cities and countries through our vast book collection, and frequently imagined myself travelling abroad to see the spectacular landmarks I pored over on the pages with my own eyes. The Eiffel Tower, the Colosseum, the Vatican, all the galleries exhibiting wonderful Renaissance art, the Brandenburg Gate, St Basil's Cathedral – I wanted to travel the world and see them all. I loved to daydream about it – maybe one day I could travel in a gondola through Venice, or walk under the Arc de

Triomphe. How amazing would that feel? But I knew I never would.

Very occasionally, Iris and Don would load us into the SUV and take us somewhere for photographs – the beach or a cliff – so that Mum could upload the posed image on to her perfect Facebook page and continue her charade; garner more hundreds and thousands of 'likes'. But these rare trips were the only time we could glimpse life in Torquay for real. I'd stared at pictures of Compington Mount in those books enough – it looked like a wild and desolate place. It held nothing much of interest. I couldn't see why the boys would ever have reason to go there.

'Okay,' I said slowly, letting the meaning of her words sink in. 'So what does that mean? That the boys might still be alive?' Why the hell would they be up there? There just wasn't enough room in my head for any more weird information, my brain was already packed full and dripping.

'It's too early for us to know any more details,' Lisa said. 'The investigation is very much ongoing and my colleagues are doing everything they can to get you answers to all this. As soon as I know anything else, of course I'll let you know straight away, Sophie. Like I said, all we know at the moment is that a signal from your father's phone was detected up around Compington Mount in the early hours of this morning. It's a start, and we can remain hopeful that it leads to something more. I do understand what a nightmare this all is for you, so in the following days and weeks please call me anytime and I'll do my very best to support you.'

I nodded. I could see – over her shoulder – that a doctor was making a beeline for my bed.

'Good morning, Sophie,' he said, as he came to a halt next to me. 'Did you sleep well?'

I nodded. The pill that the nurse had given me yesterday evening had knocked me right out.

'Great, I'm glad,' he said. He looked down at the notes pinned to his clipboard. 'Let's see. Physically, you are doing very well,' he said. 'Your wounds have been bandaged – when you're eventually discharged you'll be given fresh dressings. The deepest gashes were the most concerning, but luckily they all missed your vital organs. We know from the X-rays that you have no internal injuries, and I've looked at the results of your CT scan this morning, and you have no skull fractures or internal bleeding, which is excellent. The stab wounds on the outside of your body look much worse than what's going on on the inside. You got off very lightly, all things considered.'

I nodded. I'd seen my face in the mirror a few times when I'd gone to the bathroom, and it wasn't a pretty sight: three slashes across my face; a deep one on the left cheek, one across my forehead and a lighter one on my chin. I'd rinsed the dried clots out of my straggly hair, enjoying the sensation of becoming clean. The bandages covering the stab wounds on my skinny arms made me look like I'd been in a fight. As the doctor said, I'd got off very lightly, but I wasn't sure how, really, given what had happened to the rest of the family. I just wish I could remember something – anything. But when I tried to think back all I was met with was a haze, a blank of nothingness. It made me feel strange and horrible to know I'd survived when Rachel hadn't.

'So the thing is,' the doctor went on, looking from me to Lisa. 'There's no medical reason why we need to keep you here in the hospital any longer. But given what you've been through, it might be best for you to stay another night or two so we can keep an eye on you. What do you think, Sophie?'

What do I think? I'm not actually used to being asked my opinion on anything, so having to make any sort of decision is really hard. The truth is, I don't know what to think. I don't even know if I can look after myself, or live on my own, the thought truly scares me. I can't even remember ever going to a supermarket, although Mum probably took me when I was younger. And where am I supposed to go? Back to that house of horrors where the abuse took place? I shook my head.

'I-I don't know.' My voice came out very small.

'Why don't we think about it for a bit,' Lisa said in her friendly tones, as her eyes met mine. Ah good, someone else was taking charge. I could feel the sudden panic in me subside a bit. 'Would that be all right, Doctor, if Sophie and I mulled over your proposition for a while? She probably just needs a little time to think about the best thing to do.'

'Of course.' The doctor nodded, before turning and making his way towards another bed.

'Thanks,' I said. 'I just don't know what to do, I can't think straight.'

Lisa nodded.

'That's perfectly natural, and to be expected,' she said. 'And it's great that the only fairly bad injury you have is the deep slash on your abdomen. It means you'll make a full recovery – physically, at least. Mentally it will be a longer road, but I can put you in touch with people who can help you with that.'

I nodded, exhaling.

'Now, let's think about your options,' Lisa said, crossing her legs. 'I do have to tell you something, Sophie, and let me reassure you that there's no immediate rush for this. I don't want you to worry. But at some point, I'm going to need you to show me round your house, and point out anything that you think might be useful to this investigation. Anything that might be relevant or help us understand what led up to this ferocious attack on your family. Also, more urgently, we obviously need to locate the whereabouts of your brothers, and see if they can shed any light on who made the attack on you and your mum, dad and Rachel. Your family home has been formally searched now, but I need to understand the house from *your* perspective.

Forensics have said they've processed what they need to, so you're free to return whenever you want. After all, you know the place best. Does that make sense?'

I stared into her eyes, my heart rate intensifying in my chest, bile rising in my throat. So I was going to have to go back there, to the house that I never wanted to see again. Deep down, I'd known that I would – I mean what other real option was there? – but I'd been hoping that some magical solution would open up, and save me from having to return. However, there was a firmness in Lisa's eyes, and I knew she was serious. I'd have to go home again and show her around.

CHAPTER FOUR

R eligion started playing a part in my life for the first time as soon as I moved in with Iris and Don. We went to the local church, I attended Sunday school, and the priest would come round for tea. I'd always have to say my prayers before each meal and every night, and I had a rosary which I thought was very pretty, made out of light purple fake pearls. But after my siblings arrived, religion – or my parents' take on it – soon started dominating my life. Mum and Dad were always prominent members of the Catholic church, and at the start they'd simply seemed like fervent believers. But then they slowly ramped up their zeal inside the home rather than outside it, using it like a weapon to control us. As far as I could gather, the thing that had happened when I was little, just after the other three arrived, that caused a big problem between Mum and Dad and lots of people in their local church, really affected their thought processes. Sometimes at night, when I was supposed to be asleep, I heard them discussing their old parish. I had one memory – although I wasn't sure if this was a dream or if it really happened – of shadowy figures coming to the door one night, a low argument taking place, then my mother being even more upset than usual the next day.

The 'problem' between them and the church came to define our lives; because after they severed ties with the local priest, they set up a weird kind of church at home. Iris even made a makeshift altar in the family room, and she and Don would take it in turns being the minister behind it; giving out long sermons about hell and damnation, and how us kids better behave or the devil would take us for his own. If he did that, Iris promised, no one could save us. We'd live in eternal suffering and flames. Occasionally, her religious rantings became severe, and she would talk about God only giving us a limited time on this earth, and that when our time was up He would tell Iris and she would act accordingly. I never quite knew what she meant by that. And that our fate was determined by how good or bad we were. Once, when we'd been put to bed, I heard Iris muttering to Don downstairs about 'the wicked people from the church' and how they were 'out to get' her. I couldn't hear what Don was saying in reply, but his tone sounded soothing and placating. But then Iris said loudly, 'For goodness' sake, don't you get it? They're after *me* now. They won't rest until I'm finished.' I had no idea what she meant, or who *they* were, but I wasn't surprised Iris's façade had finally slipped and she'd fallen out with people outside of the house. She couldn't hide her true colours from everyone forever. But nothing ever happened to her, no church people ever turned up to 'finish' her off, so I forgot about it. Until the police started asking me questions about who might want to harm my parents...

In the beginning – like with all the types of abuse – it was Iris who quoted Bible passages at us first, using them to portray how wicked we were being, while Dad stayed silent and passive. He was never exactly loving towards us, but initially seemed less inclined to want to hurt or control his four kids. 'The Lord tests the righteous, but his soul hates the wicked,' I remember Mum saying. 'And I'm certainly being tested by you four ungrateful heathens. None of you realise how lucky you are, being taken in by your father and I. You'd be nothing without us, you'd be street children living in the gutter. But look at the thanks you give us, eating us out of house and home, then lying about stealing food outside mealtimes. I'm going to have to do something about that.' And she did, she put locks on the fridge and all the food cupboards so we couldn't get any snacks to soothe our aching stomachs. Because Luke and Jack were a bit overweight when they arrived, and ate like pigs because they didn't know any better, Iris decided that fatness in children disgusted her, and that it was her duty to keep us as thin as possible. Soon the boys were as reedy as Rachel and I. We were all constantly hungry, we were given such small portions at mealtimes that never filled us up. When we were very small, Dad used to sneak us up bits here and there. But Mum berated him so often about his lack of support that over the years he changed – probably to placate his waspish, beloved wife – and by the time I was nine the extra snacks had stopped.

One of Iris's favourite punishments was to withhold meals if one of us had done something to upset her. She started off making the offender just skip one plate of food, but over the years it evolved to two meals, or withholding food for a whole day or more. She would repeatedly tell us that Jesus fasted for forty days and forty nights, so the odd day here and there wouldn't do us any harm at all. The only problem was, that it did. We were still growing children, and we weren't getting enough regular nutrition.

Once, when I was six and still at school, I was so hungry one evening that I sneaked downstairs when I thought everyone was in bed and searched the kitchen for something – anything – to fill my tummy with. Eventually I looked in the bin as it was the only place I had access to as everywhere else was locked. I found some potato peelings in there and started stuffing them into my mouth wildly. I was so busy concentrating on my new food stash that I wasn't paying attention to the oncoming footsteps. Iris – coming in to get a drink of water – stopped and stared for a moment, her icy gaze taking in my gluttony. I will never forget the cold fear that swept through me as she walked towards me. She grabbed me by the hair and dragged me to the table, bending me over it, before hitting and punching my legs, back and bottom as hard as she could. 'You little pig,' she was hissing. 'You thieving beggar. Don't you ever. Ever. Do this again.' Then she quoted the Bible: '"Be on your guard against all kinds of greed".'

When I was at school the next day, changing into my shorts and T-shirt for PE like everyone else in the classroom, my teacher – Mrs Harris – came over.

'Sophie,' I remember her saying, walking round me to look at my back. 'How on earth did you get those bruises?' I remember looking at her face and it had a shocked, sad expression on it.

'I was bad, so my mum punished me,' I said. 'I should have been more like Jesus, and fasted for longer.' Mrs Harris must have reported Mum for this, because shortly afterwards a lady from social services came to our house to talk to me and Iris. Mum told her I was a rough-and-tumble child, always playing with my brothers in the garden – which wasn't true as we were never allowed to play like that because Iris didn't like noise. She told her that was how I probably got the bruises. The lady went away, and nothing seemed to come of me speaking out, except soon after that incident Mum took us all out of school. She said she was going to be our teacher now. I don't know why the school or the social services didn't look into her decision more closely, given that my bruises had already been reported. Maybe they did, and Mum manipulated her way through their questions? I was too young to know, and nothing more was ever said to me about it.

I started thinking about all of this, because I know that when I go back to my family home with Lisa, I'm going to have to look at all the sparse items Mum used to teach us with. They are all still in the 'family room', which is where my siblings and I were kept when we weren't shut in our bedrooms. I don't want to see any of that again, but it's inevitable. I know Lisa will be shocked when she sees what's inside our house, and that scares me. But we've already told the doctor that tomorrow Lisa is coming to pick me up from hospital, and is going to take me back home. So I have no choice. Tomorrow, I'm going to have to see things I never wanted to lay eyes on again.

CHAPTER FIVE

'Are you okay?' Lisa said, her eyes quickly flicking to the satnav, then back out on to the road in front. 'It looks like we're nearly at your road, Sophie. How are you feeling about going back to the house again?'

I sighed.

'Not great, to be honest.' I pulled my new hoodie tightly around myself. Lisa had brought a whole bag of new clothes to the hospital that morning. I felt so good when I put my new jeans and jumper on, I'd only ever worn threadbare charity clothes before. 'Half of me never wanted to go home again.'

Lisa nodded.

'I can only imagine how you must feel right now,' she said. 'It sounded so lonely for you there. I can't believe your parents got away with treating all of you so badly for so long. And you said you were never allowed to use any technology of any kind? Not even a computer?'

'No.' I shook my head. 'Only Iris and Don had phones and laptops. They didn't like us having any contact with the outside world. They said they were protecting us, because society is evil, and they didn't want us to fall into bad ways.'

'Hmm,' Lisa said. 'But in actual fact they were isolating you, and stopping you all telling anyone about what went on there. Classic abusive behaviour.'

I recognised the street we turned down. I'd been taken out enough to know we were one road away from Bridge Avenue, my road. Goosebumps jumped up all over my arms, and a sick feeling entered my stomach.

'We don't have to stay there too long,' Lisa said, turning the steering wheel. 'I just need you to show me round the home from your perspective. Point out anything you think might help the investigation. Also, I'm hoping it will jog your memory about the events of Sunday night and Monday morning.'

I nodded, wishing she would turn the car around and drive away.

Three minutes later, we were walking up the path towards 52 Bridge Avenue. The house of hell, as I called it in my mind.

Mr Finney, our nosy neighbour, was peeping at us through his net curtains. He was always there, watching me and my family on the rare occasions we went in and out. 'Intrusive', my dad always said about him. For all his watching, he never did anything to help us kids though. He must have known that something was off in my household, but he chose to do nothing. And when she saw him, Iris told us he was a weirdo and not to look at him – so I always obeyed her. Now, ignoring him was just a habit.

It was strange having Lisa standing next to me, opening the door with keys she said another officer had given her. Usually no one else except for me and my siblings and Iris and Don ever went into the house. Oh, and every now and again my mum's brother Oliver came round – of course, we all had to pretend to be a normal, happy family on those occasions. He'd usually arrive in the evenings, and we were all sent to bed soon after. I never got to know him. I used to listen to Oliver chatting with

Iris in the kitchen from my bed, their voices low and constant. Once I heard Dad complain to Mum about Oliver asking for money again, but that's all I know about my elusive uncle. Dad labelled him a 'layabout'. I haven't seen him for a while though.

'So, Sophie, would you like to show me around?' Lisa said, shutting the door behind us. I was standing staring at the bare hall. It smelt musty, like a few cleaning products wouldn't go amiss. Had it always smelled like this? I'd never noticed before. I looked down and saw a pile of post on the mat. The white envelope on top just had my name on it – Sophie. No address – it must have been hand-delivered. I bent down and picked it up, ripping the envelope away. I'd never had any post before. It was a card, with a picture of white roses on the front. I opened it.

Dear Sophie, I read. *I am writing to say how truly sorry I am to hear about the tragic deaths of your mother, father and sister. I'm devastated too, and am finding it hard to function. The colour has suddenly gone out of the world, and I am at a loss as I try and understand how anyone could do such an evil act. I do hope you're well on the mend too. I considered coming to visit you in hospital, but I didn't know if you'd want me there, as I know we have never had much of a chance to get to know one another. I was so sorry to hear of your injuries – the police told me all about what happened and I'm still reeling from it all. But please understand that as your uncle I am here if you need any help. Don't hesitate to contact me. Take care of yourself. Much love, Oliver.*

I stared at his scrawling writing. It was strange receiving this, I barely knew my uncle Oliver. When he occasionally popped round, my parents made sure none of us were ever left alone with him. They probably didn't want him to know the truth about their lack of parenting skills. We knew we were supposed to act like the perfect family in front of everyone else, so that's what we did in front of Oliver, just to make our own lives easier. Aren't we such a normal, perfect family, our actions used to say, as we smiled at our parents, and they ruffled our hair. And what good was it saying I should ask him if I needed help? He hadn't even written any contact details on the card.

Lisa cleared her throat, and I looked up. She smiled.

'All right?' she said. I nodded.

'Okay. Perhaps you could show me around?' she said again. I propped the card up on the hall shelf, and looked about.

I couldn't remember ever going inside anyone else's house, so I didn't know if their interiors were as bland as ours, but I thought they probably weren't. Iris didn't like me, Luke, Jack or Rachel having many possessions – or clutter – as she called it. And what we did have we were told to keep in our rooms; I shared with Rachel, and the boys slept in a different one. As I walked from the hall into the living room, Lisa following me, all we saw was a three-piece suite and a rug. Oh, and lots of bookshelves, lining every bit of wall space. The titles on there had been my saviours for all these years now – my lifeline to better opportunities – and I would be eternally grateful to them. On more than one occasion, I'd silently thanked the universe that Don and Iris – with all their many faults – were avid readers. There were a few photos on the walls; mainly of Iris and Don before we all came along – although there was one of the four of us not long after my brothers and sister arrived. We are sitting in a line, and we're all smiling. Iris was good at arranging photos, as her Facebook account shows. I can't get over how happy we were always made to look to the outside world.

Lisa was very interested in the photos, and spent a long time studying each one, asking me who was who. She also wondered whether we had any photo albums she could see, in case there were connections – other people – in them who might be helpful to talk to as part of the investigation. But I'd had to explain that no, we didn't have any albums, as far as I knew. We weren't that sort of family. But then I was never allowed to look around in Don and Iris's room. Perhaps, I suggested, they might have some in there...

'It's very tidy in here,' Lisa said, walking after me into the kitchen. This room was also characterless; just white cupboards and grey counters holding a kettle and a toaster. Like a room from a boring catalogue, rather than a real warm family home.

Lisa walked over and looked at an undone padlock – presumably formerly broken by the police – hanging off one of the cupboard doors. She reached up and opened it. Neat rows of tinned vegetables and half a loaf of bread sat on the lower shelf, and tins of soup and packets of noodles, an old peanut butter tub and jars of pasta sauce lined the upper shelf.

'So am I right in thinking that although there was plenty of food in the house, it wasn't freely available to you guys?' she said, turning. Two of the cupboards didn't have locks on, and I saw her take this in.

I nodded, hating being there again. Wishing I wasn't.

Lisa went round opening each cupboard – the police had done a good job of freeing up each lock before we'd got there. The ones that hadn't been restricted – made inaccessible – just contained boring things like lasagne sheets, dried spaghetti, pasta shells, spices and herbs and cleaning products. Okay so there *was* food in the house, but us kids didn't have free access to the edible stuff. We couldn't just go and help ourselves to snacks when we were hungry. Who likes chewing on dry, hard spaghetti? Whereas my parents ate very well, they always made sure they had balanced, healthy meals. Seafood linguine was Iris's favourite, whereas Don preferred roast beef. For years I'd had to smell their cooking, knowing I'd never be able to eat it. They generally gave us sandwiches – when they did feed us. She also looked in the fridge – cheese, ham, milk and chicken –

and the freezer – and saw a stash of neatly piled bags of frozen vegetables, slabs of meat in plastic wrappers, and a tub of sorbet. All Iris and Don's fare.

Then she turned towards me. I had no idea what she was making of all this, her face was calm and unreadable. But I wanted her to understand exactly what it had been like. It didn't look all that bad now I was showing her round; the house was in good order, it wasn't a total mess or anything. But without seeing Iris and Don in action, it was so hard to explain exactly what it had been like to all live there together.

'Come on,' she said, 'show me the rest of the house, then I'll treat you to a nice lunch.'

That sounded strange to me, as nobody had ever bought me lunch before. But it was a nice strange. I was starting to really like this woman. I think she did understand, at least partly, what I'd been through.

A minute or two later, we'd climbed the stairs to the first floor. The first small bedroom we went into was Luke and Jack's.

Lisa stopped and put her hand to her mouth. Probably because there were no beds in there, just two foam mats with no duvets or other covers. I know enough about life to know that it's not normal to make your children sleep in this way, but Iris and Don didn't care. They said it would help us stay modest and humble. Being in the boys' room made me sad, and I stepped back out on to the landing. Lisa had a look round, I could hear her opening the drawers of the little dresser. Then she joined me.

'Right, where are we going now?' she said.

'This is mine and Rachel's room,' I said, walking into an even smaller room. Again, there were two foam mats on the floor. 'I just used to wear more jumpers when it got cold,' I said, as she looked from the mats to me, a pained expression on her face. Seeing Rachel's mat made me feel very strange. For a moment a pang of sadness cut through my internal numbness unexpectedly, and I could feel tears rolling down my cheeks.

'I'm sorry to make you sad, Sophie,' Lisa said, rubbing my arm. 'Do you want to go back out while I take a quick look around?'

I nodded, wiping my eyes, retreating.

A couple of minutes later, Lisa came out of my room. She had a strange expression on her face, and I saw that she was holding something in her hand.

'Sophie, I found this phone in your room,' she said, holding it up. 'Did you know it was there?'

I stared at the old phone. I thought about lying, but what was the point? I'd tried to keep things simple up to now, so I wouldn't have to explain every little detail, but I wanted Lisa to trust me.

'Yes, I put it there,' I said, rubbing my cheek. My fingers connected with a barely healed scar and I flinched at the sudden tugging pain.

'But I thought you said that none of you were allowed to use any technology?' Lisa said.

'We weren't,' I said. 'Mum and Dad didn't know I had it.' I sighed. 'I found it. They never threw anything away. They had a few old phones locked in a drawer, but they left it open one evening so I took it and hid it. I couldn't call out on it – it says emergency calls only on the screen. But one day when they'd gone out I found out their wifi password and put it in. I didn't do much with it, just looked things up on the internet sometimes. It was my only access to the outside world, Lisa.'

Lisa stared at me.

'But why not just tell me the truth from the start?' she said. 'It's really important that you're honest with me, Sophie. I'm here to help you, but I need you to co-operate with me too. We need to work together on this. Okay?'

I nodded.

'I know,' I said. 'I'm sorry. I'm just so used to keeping everything a secret all the time. I suppose it's second nature now. And I didn't think anyone would understand why I had to stay here if I said I had it. But I won't hide anything in the future, I promise.'

Lisa looked at me, then a warm smile broke out across her face.

'Okay,' she said. 'And please know that I understand. You've had a very unusual home life and, of course, you're used to keeping everything secret from your mum and dad. I'm going to have to take this phone with me as evidence, okay?'

I nodded. I watched her take a plastic bag out of her pocket, pop my phone into it, then put it into her small shoulder bag.

'Right,' she said. 'Carry on with the tour.'

I did, I showed her my mum and dad's bedroom with its big double bed complete with fluffy duvet and pillows. Lisa tutted as she looked at it and muttered something about how monstrous it was that they should give themselves a normal bed when they made their kids sleep on mats. She had a good look round in there, in the wardrobe and drawers, under the bed. I had to go and stand outside on the landing again while she was doing that – I'd had it drummed into me for so long that I should never snoop around my parents' belongings that I felt shameful even being in there. She wasn't holding anything when she came out, so presumably she didn't find anything of interest.

Then we went into the bathroom, then the small 'family room' my siblings and I were often locked in – complete with its low table, or 'altar'. Its small whiteboard and pens, the bookshelves stacked with 'educational' material. But the whole time I was feeling strange, guilty that she'd found my hidden phone. I wanted Lisa to like me, I'm not sure why. She was just so normal and nice, and now she'd found that I hadn't been completely honest with her. But how could I be? She just wouldn't understand. No one would. And there were other things she didn't know. Things that I'd started to remember about that night, that my brain had hidden from me when I first got to hospital. But how would she react if and when she found out about them? Now that she had my phone she would find out some of the things I'd been doing, things I never wanted anyone to know. I needed to be more careful...

CHAPTER SIX

I never told Iris or Don that I'd stopped believing in God years ago. That would have been inviting the worst whipping of my life, and probably no food for at least a week. But privately I just didn't see how this wonderful God that Iris told us about could possibly exist, given the state of my life. Iris told us that God didn't love us when we were bad, that He only loved us when we did what she and Dad said because then we were being good. 'Honour your father and your mother', she always said. And until I was twelve, I really did believe in the Almighty, and I tried my hardest every day to be good for him, and to honour and respect my parents. We had to learn Bible passages every day and one of my favourites was 'Ask and it will be given to you; seek and you will find', because every night all I asked God for were parents who loved me and treated me well. But He never listened, and I knew from the way that Iris and Don treated me that they didn't love me at all. On my thirteenth birthday, Iris accused me of putting on weight, and she said I must have been secretly stealing food and eating it, which just wasn't true. I was as starving as usual, and had no idea why I looked less skinny than normal. Perhaps puberty was trying to kick in, albeit with no nourishment. But Iris was so angry she forbade my siblings or Don from saying happy birthday to me. I started properly hating her after that, I didn't think God would love Iris as she was such a bitch. So in the end I concluded that religion was a load of crap and that my mum and dad were using it as one of their tools to control us with.

But even so, some of the things they'd banged into us stayed in my mind and confused me. Like the outside world being evil. Iris showed us so many newspaper articles about terrible murders and drug addicts and bad things that went on, that part of me really *did* believe the world outside the house was a very bad place. She also told me and Rachel that we would go to hell if we ever had boyfriends, as God hated hussies and sluts. Once, about two years ago, when Iris had taken me and Rachel to a park to take photos of us for her Facebook page, a group of boys came and stood near the swings we were sitting on. One of them smiled at me, and for a moment I felt really good. He had a nice face. Then this ice-cold fear washed through me as I remembered what Iris had said about hussies. I've thought about that moment a lot. By my logic, if God doesn't exist then everything Iris said about him hating sluts is null and void. So why can I never shake the shame of that moment? Luckily Iris didn't see him smile at me, she was too busy staring at her phone.

I'd stolen Dad's old phone from the drawer that time because I'd felt so alone to the point that I was going mad, and I needed some sort of lifeline to the outside world. I needed to see what other people's lives were like; what teens my age were up to. I was too scared to use it for ages, in case Iris or Don caught me, but then I got braver and once I connected it to the wifi I started searching the internet. To begin with, I wasn't looking for anything in particular, I was just stunned with the huge amount of information suddenly available to me. Finding things out made me hate my mum and dad even more, knowing they were keeping us away from so much good stuff as well as from the bad. I found out about all the social media sites, gazed at other teenagers who looked so much more mature and more confident than me. It made me so jealous of them, although I knew it wasn't their fault, of course. They just had normal parents.

After a few months, I'd made myself a Facebook account, under a false name. My new alias was Melody Brown. At first, I just browsed other people's accounts, as well as – naturally – repeatedly checking out my mother's sham one, and slowly people started friending me, which felt absolutely amazing. I was a real person! I mattered! Then I got a bit braver, and posted a few pictures of animals and nature that I'd found on the internet. Then one day, I posted a photo of my face. That's when he first contacted me. Zach Trydell. He sent me a private message, saying he thought I was pretty. I couldn't believe it; I was so pleased but I was even more scared. If Iris knew what I was doing she'd probably kill me. I didn't reply to Zach for several days, because I was internally wrestling with the thought of being a slut and going to hell. But in the end, I did. And that was how our friendship first began.

CHAPTER SEVEN

L isa and I were back downstairs in the living room when her phone rang.

I watched her face as she listened and spoke. It was looking more and more serious, concerned.

'Right,' she was saying. 'I see. No, that's not good news, is it. Okay, thanks for letting me know. I'll pass the information on to Sophie.'

As she put her phone back into her pocket, Lisa turned her big brown eyes towards me. There was sorrow in them.

'Let's sit down for a minute.' She gestured towards the sofa. I already knew what she was going to say – gut feeling – but I sat down anyway.

'I'm so sorry to tell you this, Sophie, but when my colleagues were searching Compington Mount, they found a body.'

The now familiar nausea shot up my throat and I doubled over.

'Which one of them is it?' I said through clenched teeth.

Lisa sighed.

'They believe the body is Luke's,' she said. 'Although they

are waiting for confirmation. He has a large birthmark on the back of the neck, does that sound at all familiar to you?'

I nodded.

'It's Luke.' The room swam in front of me. I shut my eyes as pain once again pierced through the numbness in me. 'What about Jack?'

'Jack still hasn't been found.' Lisa's voice was soft. 'But under the circumstances I have to tell you to prepare yourself for the worst, Sophie. All this is very unusual, and I can reassure you that the police are working as hard as they can to make sense of all of it. We need to understand why Luke's body ended up on Compington Mount, away from the car, cliff and the rest of you. It's a good three miles away. CCTV clearly shows that you were all in the car together at the beginning of the evening, at approximately twenty to seven, but now a more complex scenario is playing out, and we all need to work as a team to put the jigsaw pieces back together. You've already told my colleagues about anyone you know who might wish your mother and father harm, and they are looking into their connections with the local church. But so far, nothing significant has come to light. So we need to dig deeper. We need to find Jack.'

I rocked gently back and forth on the edge of the sofa, my mind in a tailspin. Poor Luke, the quietest of us four. He didn't deserve to be murdered, no way. The thing was, my strange brain – that had initially protected me from remembering anything – had started filtering through a few cold, hard facts about Sunday night. Not everything, but flashes here and there. And so I *knew* it just didn't make any logical sense that Luke would end up on the mount. Up until that moment I'd even convinced myself that I'd lost my memory – it was just easier. I didn't want to accept what I was remembering. It had been much better in the hospital when my mind was a proper blank.

But seriously, Luke couldn't be up there. It shouldn't – couldn't – be possible – not with what I knew. This was all so horrendously fucked up. But there was no way I could tell Lisa – or anyone else – about what I actually remembered. No way at all. The gravity of the mess I was now in hit me with the force of a gunshot. A thin layer of fear took over everything else inside me; the horror, the relief of feeling somewhat better than I ever had, the sadness about Luke, Rachel and Jack. Things had just got complicated, and I couldn't distance myself; whichever way I thought about it, I was involved with circumstances that scared me...

CHAPTER EIGHT

I'd lied to Iris and Don on Monday afternoon, hours before the accident. So in a way, all that had happened was my fault. Without meaning to, I'd initiated a big change in our lives that had led to all this destruction. I'd told them I'd reported them to social services on Rachel's behalf. I told them I'd stolen a phone and taken pictures of the bruises on Rachel's front, back, arms and legs and emailed them to someone. I hadn't taken any photos, but I wanted to make them worry and stop treating us so badly. Dad had beaten her the week before, because she was refusing to read the Bible. She kept telling him she was too exhausted to sit up, but he didn't care. In the end, Mum told him to correct her behaviour, so he did. By punching and hitting her. So I told Mum and Dad that social services would be coming the next day to check on Rachel, and that when they saw the bruises in real life they would probably take us all away. And then Mum and Dad would have to go to prison, and that we would all testify against them because we HATED them. That they would be locked up for the rest of their lives, which I'd be glad about. I said I hoped they would rot in their cells forever. It was a big moment for me, doing this. I'd never stood up to them before in such a way, never taken an assertive step to call them out on how they treated us. I mean, I'd resisted punishments – moved when Iris slapped me, turned my head when Don poured water over my face. But this was the first time I'd felt strong enough to try and actually stop them in their tracks, and I had Zach to thank for my transformation in mental strength.

I've never seen Don really lose his shit before. I've seen Iris go mad plenty of times, but Dad was always the calmer, more composed one, even when he was whipping us. But not this time. He went straight to the drinks cabinet, undid the lock, then poured himself a glass full of straight whisky. He necked the whole thing in one go. Mum was doing her low screaming thing at me; low enough for the neighbours not to hear or be worried, but shrill enough to make my ears hurt. She told me I was a selfish ungrateful little cow, and that she wished they'd never adopted me, that I'd brought them nothing but trouble.

I knew Iris would be angry, I didn't know Don would react like that, but to be honest – I didn't actually care. Becoming friends with Zach had given me the confidence to stand up to my mum and dad for once. And when I did, it felt so good. To be accurate – Zach had given me the confidence. Slowly, as we chatted online over the weeks and months, I told him about my life, little by little. He said my situation was insane, he called it abusive. I was shocked at first, because I was so used to it, it felt normal. But when Zach told me about his life, and how his parents showed their love for him and had encouraged him to do normal things all his life, like have friends round, go on school trips and practise different sports, I started to realise how fucked up my own world actually was.

I didn't say swear words until I got to know Zach. Only Mum and Dad were allowed to swear whenever they felt like it in our house; we would get beaten if we dared say anything like that. Luke said 'shit' once, when he dropped a china bowl on his toes and it broke, and Iris grabbed him by the hair, took him over to the sink and ran water from the tap all over his face until he couldn't breathe. Swearing at home really wasn't worth the bother. But Zach wrote swear words in his messages to me, not bad ones, but things like '*I can't be fucked to work today*', or '*my brother is pissing me off*'. I kind of liked it actually, and I started to *think* in swear words sometimes, especially when I was feeling brave or angry.

It was Zach who told me I should threaten Iris and Don with social services to scare them. He said they could do with a taste of their own medicine, and be the terrified ones for once, instead of bullying us. I wouldn't have had the courage to go through with it without him. Even though I've never actually met him, I feel protected by Zach, I know he cares about me and he's looking out for me. He looks gorgeous in his photos. I need to find a way to log back on to Facebook, but Lisa's taken my phone. A claustrophobic feeling descended over me, and for a moment I felt like I was drowning in the air in the room. All I wanted to do was see Zach's photo, to read a reassuring message from him; he'd tell me everything was going to be okay and then my nerves would calm down and everything would seem better. I now didn't care whether being friends with him made me a slut or hussy in the eyes of God; my feelings for him were too overwhelming. But how the hell could I reach him?

CHAPTER NINE

'I want to go up to Compington Mount,' I said. I stood up and wiped my eyes. 'I want to go now. Please, Lisa.' As soon as she'd told me about Luke, I'd become swamped by a desire to see – with my own eyes – where my poor brother was found. It would be some sort of reality check, I felt. At the moment, nothing seemed very tangible – almost like people were making all this horrific stuff up about my family. I needed concrete proof that this all wasn't just a bad dream...

Lisa paused. She looked as though she was thinking.

'Okay,' she said. 'Come on, I'll drive you up there.'

Ten minutes later we had driven out of the residential part of Torquay and were winding our way up a steep road. There were no houses there, just increasingly wild undergrowth on either side of the car, with trees and brambles creating walls of foliage. It made me feel desolate, imagining Luke dying in a place like this, away from anyone who cared about him. I willed the numbness inside me to get stronger – I didn't want to feel anything. Emotions now scared me, they had proven to be too powerful to handle.

The first thing I noticed, when we'd left the car on the side of the road and I'd followed Lisa through the messy woodland to the edge of a crevice, was a bedraggled media crew. The whole area around them smelled of earthy dampness. The photographers and reporters were ignoring the drizzle and craning for the best view. They were peering down one of the sides of the mount, amid twisted trees – two weirdly entwined together – and thorny brambles. At first, I couldn't see what they were looking at, and a shot of anger went through me – because they were looking at the site of my brother's death before me. Some of them were laughing and talking with each other, and their uncaring behaviour just felt rude. I walked forward, pushing roughly through the crowd, making sure I elbowed a couple of people unnecessarily hard.

Then I stopped.

About a metre below me were four people wearing white forensic suits. They were walking around a body bag, studying the ground. My brother was in that bag. Luke – the serious, quiet boy who always tried his best to look after me and Rachel. He didn't deserve to end up like this. I didn't want to look at him in the bag, but I couldn't tear my eyes away.

'Hi, Sophie?' a familiar voice said. I made myself move my gaze, and found it was one of the police officers who'd come to see me at the hospital talking. Detective Warner.

I raised a limp hand. It was supposed to be a greeting, as I couldn't talk.

I felt Lisa arrive next to me.

'Sophie wanted to come up here as soon as I told her the news,' she said to Detective Warner. 'I thought it might help her process everything that's happened if she saw the scene.'

'Yes,' Detective Warner said. It was only now that I noticed the other person who'd been at the hospital – I think Lisa had said his name was Detective Pierce. As usual, he was standing quite far away, watching me. Always the observer. 'Perhaps.

This must be hard for you, Sophie? I'm so sorry about your brother. I'm afraid I can't let you come any closer, as we're still processing everything. Is that okay?'

I nodded. I was staring at the ground around the body bag – at least at the patches I could see that weren't being trodden on. The area looked messy, like someone had emptied a rubbish bag everywhere. I saw Luke's beloved pocket Bible lying open under a couple of leaves. It looked damp, and some of the pages were ripped. He'd always been a much better pseudo-Catholic than me; even when Iris and Don were evil to him, he kept his faith and prayed even harder. He really believed, and I hoped this would stand him in good stead now, that he would be happy in a much better place. They let Luke have the Bible as one of his only possessions, because they approved of it. I'd recognise it anywhere, because my brother had stuck the well-used pages back together so many times with tape. I could see bits of it sticking up here and there. I jumped down, wanting to touch it – pick it up.

'I'm afraid I can't let you handle anything here, Sophie love,' Detective Warner said quickly, putting her arms out in a low defensive gesture. 'This is a crime scene, and it's important that none of the items here are contaminated, just in case we need to use them as evidence.'

I looked at her.

'How did Luke die?' I said.

'We're still not sure,' Detective Warner said, her face serious. 'A forensic post-mortem will be performed – probably later today – in order to confirm the manner of death. But please prepare yourself as at the moment it looks like a homicide – murder. Lisa here will keep you updated about any developments.' She gave a small smile, but her eyes remained grave.

I nodded. Then I looked down again, at the mess among the

twigs and leaves. Old crisp packets, a half empty bottle of water, three crushed lager cans. A burnt patch of ground that had some sort of fire on it. Then something else caught my eye, and I craned to see it better. It looked familiar, but it shouldn't have been up Compington Mount with Luke's body. I took another step forward, and Detective Warner put her arms out again to stop me from going any further.

Stuck in a muddy patch near the trunk of a tree, was a gold cigarette lighter. I'd seen it before, when my uncle Oliver came over. It was very distinctive – a Zippo lighter I think he called it. It looked like a small metal box with a lid. Mum had always made him go out into the garden to smoke, and I remember watching him crack the lid of the lighter back, and a large flame rearing up towards the cigarette in his mouth. A petrol-like smell would then fill the air, just before his first nicotine waft took it over. Hang on, Sophie, I said to myself. There must be more than one Zippo lighter in the world. His has an engraving of a dragon on it. I bet this one doesn't. Even though I knew Detective Warner didn't want me to go any further, I took a deep breath and lunged forward. I really badly needed to know if this was my uncle's lighter. As the detective started protesting, I bent down. I had just enough time to see the faint dragon engraving on the side of the lighter before she pulled me away.

CHAPTER TEN

So, if I'm really honest, I have to admit that my siblings and I had a bit more freedom at home than I've let on to Lisa and the other police. I find lying really easy – even to myself – and I'm trying to keep details simple for them, black and white, so my situation and upbringing is easy for them to understand. We were all like this, my brothers, sister and I, it was a survival strategy. We honestly wouldn't have been able to do *anything* at all, if we hadn't become experts at covert – dishonest – behaviour; hiding things from Iris and Don's eyes.

As Lisa now knows, I found my tiny bit of freedom through technology. I loved surfing the internet when everyone else was asleep. It always blew me away – how you can find anything out about any subject in the world nowadays. So I took full advantage of that. I researched nature and different countries, different types of music – my favourite is the blues – celebrities, crime around the world, psychology, law, you name it, I looked it up. I watched free documentaries on YouTube, and learnt more than I ever had about the world through them. My brothers' bit of freedom – on the other hand – all started when they realised they could get in and out of their bedroom window at night without Iris and Don realising.

It was Jack who'd made friends with Uncle Oliver first. He used to go and chat to him while Oliver was dragging away on his cigarette in the garden – with Mum staring at them from the back door. I think Oliver felt sorry for my brothers, he probably imagined himself being a teenage boy with no freedom. So one day he whispered to them to stay up that night, then open their window when our parents – both heavy sleepers – were slumbering. They did just that, and Oliver was standing in the front garden. He told them how to jump out without hurting themselves. I don't know what they all did out there, but I know it involved smoking because early the next day, the boys asked me to secretly wash the clothes they'd been wearing so Mum and Dad didn't smell the smoke. From then on, they'd jump down and spend time with Oliver on a fairly regular basis. Not that often, maybe once or twice a month. When I thought about it, I guess my uncle must have given Luke his lighter, which is why it was found up on Compington Mount. I don't think Oliver had anything to do with Luke being there, he's not that sort of person. A bit weak-minded, but not violent like Mum. Oh my God, I really feel like I'm living in a dream... or a nightmare...

Poor little Rachel had the least freedom out of all of us. The problem with her was that she was too full of fear, while me, Luke and Jack were rebels at heart. She'd probably still be alive today if she'd been able to stand up to my parents for once in her life... I tried to help her do that on Sunday night, I really did... I've remembered that part now...

CHAPTER ELEVEN

'Lovely Local Family Found Stabbed to Death in Their Car', the *Daily News* headline read. 'And Their Son's Death is Being Treated as Suspicious. One More Teen Still Missing...' Lovely family, I thought. Sure. What a load of crap. Ah, there was a photo of Luke in his body bag on Compington Mount. How morbid. And the famous one that went viral of me and Brianna Salotto at the Destruction Revolution rally, with dear Iris in the background. And an absolutely horrific snap of the bloodied SUV's interior after the bodies of my family had been removed. I looked away. I didn't want to see that at all.

It was Thursday, the day after Luke's body was found. Lisa brought the paper with her when she came to see me.

I'd had quite a good morning up to that point; there was something rather freeing about getting up by myself, with no Iris, Don or anyone else around to ruin my day. The horrible, constricting feeling that had overwhelmed me yesterday had dissipated with a long sleep; I'd been dead to the world for hours. I still yearned for contact with Zach, but had internally talked myself into a better perspective about all that; surely there were public computers I could use – maybe at the library or something? Feeling better, I'd even popped to the corner shop to get some bread and milk, as well as some disinfectant and a packet of cloths – my first time ever doing that. Of course, I was still traumatised about my siblings, but I was also experiencing a calmness on the inside that I'd never had before. The previous night, I'd held my own little ceremony for poor Rachel and Luke, and even for missing Jack. Nothing religious of course, just a remembrance kind of thing. I'd found a little drawing of a flower that Rachel had done with biro on a piece of notepaper, a buckle that had fallen off Luke's belt that he kept by the side of his mat, and a comb that Jack used. I'd stared at all of them on the counter, said my goodbyes to Luke and Rachel, told Jack he needed to be found. I currently had all these keepsakes in my pocket; I felt better for having them close to me. I knew Lisa had been kind to bring me the paper, so I forced my attention back to the sickening article.

Why did this happen to the Macreavy family? I continued to read. *Iris and Don Macreavy were upstanding members of the community, heavily involved with their church, always the first to delve deep into their pockets for charitable causes. They'd adopted four children – two boys and two girls – and built a happy home. Don's business, DM Printing Services, had gone from strength to strength, allowing the family a comfortable way of life. Iris, a stay-at-home mother who home-schooled their children, posted many happy snaps of their perfect family life on her Facebook account. So what went wrong? How did three of the Macreavys end up fatally stabbed in their blue SUV on top of Meadcoombe Cliff in the early hours of Monday morning? Another member of the family, nineteen-year-old Sophie, was also found stabbed in the car and required immediate medical care. The police haven't released many details, and say their investigations are ongoing. To make a tragic situation even worse, the couple's seventeen-year-old son Luke was found dead up on Compington Mount yesterday. His autopsy results are not yet known but initial signs are that his death is being treated as suspicious. Luke's twin, Jack, is still missing. Police say he is definitely a person of interest in both cases and are asking him to come forward, in order to help them with their investigations...*

What the actual hell? I let the newspaper sag downwards as I tried to get my head round the utter drivel written about my family. What lies, what distortion. There were several photos of us kids printed too, all taken from Mum's Facebook page. No wonder people think we were the perfect family, I'd think so, too, if all I had to go on were these photos. At first glance we look so wholesome together, always doing some activity like walking through leaves, or hugging, or gazing at the sea. But if you look closer at our eyes, you can tell the smiles are not real. Or maybe it's just me who can see that, because I know the truth. And the one of Brianna and I, with Iris looking on, just solidifies the lie she perpetrated; the charade of us being so wholesome, caring and close as a family. Contrasted with the bloodied car scene; the whole thing did look like an utterly awful tragedy. And it was, in more ways than one. But we hadn't been a 'lovely' family at all. That part was a heinous lie. A mistaken perception that was just too much for me to swallow. Anger bubbled up in me as I looked at the fakeness of the photos. How dare Iris use us like that? How could she care so little about who we were on the inside? It made me so mad. I'm glad she's dead.

If I'm honest, I didn't actually know what was going to happen on Sunday night, when Dad made everyone get into the car. I mean, not really. It wasn't like I had an actual plan or anything...

CHAPTER TWELVE

Lisa also brought a new phone for me when she came over this morning with the paper. I was so happy when I saw it, I kept saying thank you to her. I'd never been given anything new like that, it instantly became my favourite ever possession. I actually couldn't keep the happy grin off my face. I didn't want to seem rude and start using it when she was there, but as soon as she'd gone I opened the box and read the instruction leaflet from start to finish. I was desperate to talk to Zach, and was so grateful that Lisa had given me this unexpected lifeline. Soon, I'd put in the SIM card and was charging it up. I lay on the carpet for ages, gazing at its beautiful blue screen, watching the little charging bars continuously go up, then back down – up, then back down – in the corner of it. My very own phone. And it was a gift. No one would ever take it off me or punish me for having it. And soon I'd be talking to my beautiful friend once again...

But still, something about Lisa's attitude towards me seemed to have shifted today. Or maybe I was imagining it? She seemed a little more distant, not quite as smiley. She was still nice though, and asked if there was anything else I needed, whether

I'd like her to help me do a few basic things like make a dentist appointment, or buy new toiletries, or get hold of some recipe books – even come to the supermarket with me. She asked how I was finding it – living in the house by myself – and I told her it wasn't as bad as I'd been expecting. That I was slowly getting used to it, and actually it was kind of peaceful now that Iris and Don weren't here shouting at everyone. She'd nodded at that point, and said she understood. It was kind of a relief when she'd left though.

I'm probably imagining that she's being distant. After all, the psychiatrist at the hospital who came to talk to me before I left said I might well experience some post-traumatic stress symptoms as a result of everything I'd been through. He said these can include hypervigilance – where you are so alert and sensitive to everything around you, you can feel almost paranoid. So it's probably just that. I haven't done anything I need to worry about, so I have to try and relax and start looking forward to the future. I still can't think about Rachel or Luke, or even about Jack – which is why I'm glad I have the wonderful numbness in me that blocks out my feelings most of the time. Yesterday's overwhelming fear was awful, but I think I was overreacting. I mean, the memories about what happened that night – that keep coming back bit by bit – are just in my head. It's not like anyone else is going to find out about them, as long as I keep playing it cool. Don't say anything more than I need to.

So I can't tell Lisa that I remember us all getting into Dad's SUV on Sunday evening. Me, Rachel, Luke, Jack, Iris and Don. Dad made us get in, after he'd had two more whiskys. He had his belt in his hand, but he didn't need to use it, we were all too well trained. He was acting like he'd lost his mind, I'd never seen him so frantic. Even Mum was staring at him like she couldn't believe her eyes. He said we needed to get away from the house for a while, that there was no way we were going to stay and let ourselves be torn to shreds by social services. I was enjoying his pain actually. It felt good to see him so upset and worried instead of it being me strung out to my last nerve, like usual. That might sound heartless, but it was a kind of revenge. He deserved to know how it felt – to feel out of control, and at the mercy of someone else's actions.

It was when he'd driven out of our road, and on to the main road, that things inside our car suddenly changed...

CHAPTER THIRTEEN

I honestly had no idea where Jack was. I certainly hadn't remembered anything about that, and I don't think I will. He was meant to survive, they all were; my siblings. That was the whole point. I was trying to help them as well as me by threatening our parents. We *all* deserved better treatment, not just me. If he still had Dad's new phone in his possession – while I had the old one I'd nicked out of the drawer – then maybe, just maybe, he would answer if I rang it...

I didn't know Dad's number off by heart, so it took me a while to find it. Don and Iris rarely threw anything away, I knew the box Dad's phone came in must still be in the house somewhere, so I went into their bedroom to start looking. I opened their wardrobe and immediately felt sick. All the clothes inside smelt of them. Urgh, I got a whiff of Iris's perfume from somewhere. It was disgusting, shame washed through me as it always did when I was near Mum or Dad. They'd spent so many years making it obvious that I was less than them, that I was nothing more than a dirty little animal they'd saved from a druggie mother. I couldn't shake the feeling that they might be right, that I might be a subhuman person who was pretty worthless. But today I couldn't pay attention to those feelings, I had to find Dad's number. And it angered me that they were coming back, I'd been feeling so much better in myself recently. Most of the time. Okay, yesterday had been pretty awful...

I searched through the neatly stacked belongings at the bottom of the wardrobe, putting several things aside to look at in more detail later. A large black rucksack – barely used, a pile of old diaries, boxes of photographs showing Mum's life before we came along, Dad's old work files, and dusty bundles of letters. No phone box. I stood up and went over to their shiny mahogany dresser, pulling open each drawer and rummaging through the contents. This was the first ever time in my life that I'd been able to root around in Iris and Don's room, and I felt half guilty, half thrilled that I was doing it. I kept expecting one of them to come in and shout at me, but of course, that would never happen again now. I could spend as long in there as I wanted.

The top three drawers contained underwear, tops and jumpers, but the bottom drawer – the largest – turned out to be a storage space for odds and ends. I took out an old pencil case, a broken alarm clock, a tissue box with no tissues left in it and three books about religion. Then right at the bottom, next to a pile of half-used hair-conditioner bottles, I saw two boxes. I pulled them both out. I soon realised they were *both* phone boxes, used to house different mobile phones at one time or other. Now that was confusing. I studied the information on the sides of each, trying to work out what box matched Don's most recent device. I was never allowed to use it, but I'd seen him with it often enough. It was black, with a large screen, like my new one. I looked at the pictures on the sides of the boxes and soon realised which was the correct one. The other phone looked older and had a keypad. I put everything back in the drawer, then jogged back down the stairs, excited about finding

Dad's telephone number on the back of the box, eager to punch it into my own phone, but terrified about what I might hear if anyone answered.

Seconds later, I'd finished tapping the number in, and pressed the green handset symbol. I watched and waited, then my heart jumped when I heard a ringing sound. Dad's phone must be turned on... Then someone answered. I nearly dropped my phone but I fumbled quickly and brought it up to my ear.

'Hello?' I said. 'Jack? Is that you? This is Sophie. Are you okay?' I stopped, and listened. But all I could hear on the other end were slow, heavy breaths. The ice-cold fear was suddenly back in my brain with a vengeance...

CHAPTER FOURTEEN

Lisa didn't know I was listening to her phone conversation. I may not be an expert at many things, but I could get a degree in covert secrecy. I was – ostensibly – looking at my new phone at the kitchen table, very kindly given to me by Lisa and bought with money from the police victims' fund. I'd *finally* got back in touch with Zach last night, after putting in the wifi code from Iris and Don's modem. It was so good to speak to him again. I told him all about the weird call I'd made to Dad's phone, and he told me not to worry, that it probably signalled that Jack was still alive, which was a great sign. The battery might have run out, he'd said. If he's lost or unwell he wouldn't be able to find a charger for it. Zach had said it sounded like so many police were out looking for him that he would be found soon. He also said he'd been really worried about me, especially when he read about what had happened to my parents and sister in the papers. He kept asking if I was okay, he really is the sweetest person. I care about him so much; I actually can't stop thinking about him. I wonder when we can meet face to face? Seeing as I'm a free agent now, that shouldn't be a problem. There's no one who can stop me from living my life now...

But despite Zach's reassurances, I can't stop thinking about the weird call I'd had with Dad's phone yesterday. I'm sure it's a good sign that Jack's still alive, but I'd only heard that awful breathing, no one had actually said anything. Then suddenly, whoever it was – Jack? – hung up, and when I tried to call back the phone had been turned off. The panic I felt initially subsided when Zach talked me through it. But still. It reminded me of the horror of all of this; it sliced through the niceness of Zach, through the numbness I like having in my brain. I can't bear to think of my brother out there, hurt, alone, or wherever he is. But also, I'm beginning to realise that there's a part of me that likes it without my siblings around. I know that sounds bad and heartless, but it's true. If Jack is found, what state will he be in? Will I have to give my whole life over to looking after him? Then my new freedom will end, and honestly, I would hate that. Don't get me wrong, it doesn't mean I wish them harm. I don't at all. I just feel, what's the word? Ambivalent. Undecided, about which would be the better life; to have my siblings around, or to just be a lone wolf and look after myself without worrying about anyone else.

I didn't tell Lisa I'd made the call, in case I'd done something I shouldn't have. My default state of mind is to think I'm always in trouble, and that everything I do is wrong. So I've just got used to not telling other people what I'm up to in case I'm punished. But I'd been thinking about how to find Jack since, and I'd tried to phone back so many times – but Dad's phone was now permanently turned off. Where the hell was my brother? I wasn't sure how I felt about him being found in an awful state, but not knowing was like torture all the same... Bloody hell, I'm such a conflicted person. Although at least I'm coming to terms with that now...

'I know,' Lisa was saying. She was standing in the hall near the front door, obviously thinking she was far enough away from my good hearing. 'I don't know what's really happened to Sophie in the past. I saw those videos she posted on YouTube too, when forensics were looking at her old phone. She'd been making them for months before the accident happened... Yep... Yeah, I agree with you. Something's just not adding up here. She's painted the most awful picture of her home life, and don't get me wrong, I think it was bad in places, after all, the kids were forced to sleep on mats. But she also told me she had no access to technology, yet then I find out she has a phone and has been making videos on YouTube... Also, she's not displaying typical grief about the loss of her family, not even for Rachel, who she says she was really close to. Half the time she doesn't even seem that interested in the investigation... No, I don't think she'll tell me the truth if I ask her straight out... Okay, I'll keep working on it... Bye.'

I bent my head over my phone as she came back in, pretending to be absorbed with my new gadget.

'Hi again,' Lisa said, sitting down at the table opposite me. 'That was Detective Pierce, just giving me an update. The autopsy report has come back, and I'm afraid that the coroner has found that Luke's death was compression of the neck. He was murdered. I'm so sorry, Sophie.'

I looked at her. She was watching me carefully.

'That's awful,' I said. I meant it. The only thing was that I couldn't feel anything because of my numb, emotionless internal system. I thought of Zach and wished I could tell him the news straightaway, so he could tell me everything was okay again. Is there something wrong with me? Why don't I react and cry, like normal people would, when someone tells them such tragic news?

'Yes, it is,' Lisa said slowly. 'And there's still no sign of Jack. Given the results of the post-mortem, the investigation into

Luke's death is now a murder one. You do understand that, don't you, Sophie?'

'Yes,' I said, nodding.

'Everyone who is still alive and who knew Luke will be interviewed, because the police need to work out who wanted him to die,' Lisa said, her big brown eyes trained on me. 'That means you will be called in to the police station too. Okay?'

'Yes.' I nodded again. 'I understand.'

Lisa sat back and I heard a low exhaling sound come out of her mouth.

'I must say, Sophie. You are taking the news about Luke's murder remarkably calmly. Were you close to him?'

'Um,' I said, tingles of real fear dancing in my head as I realised she was wondering whether I was involved somehow. Then suddenly a massive block of terror arrived. 'Yeah. Sort of. It was hard to be close to anyone in this house, Lisa. We were all kept silent, we weren't allowed to talk with each other that much. But I cared about him. I hated seeing him or my other siblings punished or hurt.' Shit. A very bad feeling was now in the pit of my stomach.

Lisa stared at me.

'Of course,' she said. 'Well, I'll let you know when you are going to be interviewed. Okay?'

'Yep,' I said, watching her stand up.

'I'll pop in again tomorrow,' Lisa said, reaching down to get her bag. 'Sleep well, Sophie. Don't forget to cook some of that food I brought you. I don't think you've been using much of the money I gave you to gather supplies, have you? You're nothing but skin and bone. You need to get used to eating bigger meals.' She smiled, but it wasn't with the same warmth as usual. My heart felt sad all of a sudden. I'd enjoyed her being nice to me. I wanted her to like me. But if she didn't it was my fault – as usual – for being weird and secretive and messing everything up.

'I will,' I said. 'Thanks, Lisa. For all your help and support.'

'No worries at all,' Lisa said, her tone bright. 'That's what I'm here for.'

We said our goodbyes, and seconds later, she was gone.

I picked up my phone, and typed *Lisa Denton family liaison officer* into Google. I wanted to know more about this woman who'd suddenly become such a big part of my life. She knew so much about me, yet I knew absolutely nothing about her...

CHAPTER FIFTEEN

Thanks to my hours of late-night Google researching over the last few months, I knew how to get what I wanted from the internet pretty easily. At first, just a local newspaper article from a few years ago popped up and I saw the phrase, *Officer Lisa Denton (20) joins the Devon and Cornwall family liaison team.* I clicked on it, and saw it was just a short bit about general police recruitment, with a photo of Lisa in uniform at the top. Next, I tried Facebook – and it turns out that there are hundreds of Lisa Dentons around the world. So I decided to narrow my search down using location keywords. Ah, there she was – with her unmistakeable brown hair and pretty face. Her account name was Lisa Jane. Her page must have privacy settings on it as I couldn't access much information, but in her profile photo she had her arm round a tall man with big muscles and a shaved head. Both of them smiling, they made a cute couple. I clicked on the photo and saw that she'd tagged someone in called Jason Stewart. That must be her partner; I don't think they're married as I had a good look at her ring finger when she was last here.

I clicked on Jason's Facebook page, and it was much more

open and accessible than Lisa's – with loads of photos of him and Lisa doing different things; drinking with friends, camping, at the seaside, pulling funny faces. They seemed to have a great life, did so much together. Ah, and one of them both in police uniform; so he was a police officer too.

I tried to ignore the jealous jolt that looking at these photos gave my insides. I should be pleased for Lisa that she had such a good life; a good career, a relationship, perfect looks, and freedom. I bet her childhood was fantastic as well, not like the shitshow mine's been. But I couldn't help asking myself: how is this fair that she gets her life, and I get mine? Why should she get all the happiness, and me all the crap stuff? For a minute, I wondered what I'd be like if I'd grown up in Lisa's shoes – been given all the love and opportunities she had. I think I'd be a better, nicer person than I am. I know I'm selfish, and I know I've got a dark side. But I can't help it. It's the only way I know how to be. It's probably why I'm not more upset about Rachel or Luke dying. I know it's sad, and that they didn't deserve what happened to them. But I'm just relieved I'm alive myself, and that I'm not living with Iris and Don anymore. Does that sound really bad and self-centred? Still, I'm scared now. On high alert, aware that Lisa's opinion of me has changed. She thinks something isn't right about me. Something's off. Maybe she's right, but it isn't what she thinks...

CHAPTER SIXTEEN

'Why did you make those YouTube videos, Sophie?'
Lisa's voice was stern, her eyes unsmiling. It felt like a completely different woman was in my house than the one who'd introduced herself to me in the hospital. It was Saturday morning, and we were sitting opposite each other at the kitchen table.

'I've already told you,' I said. 'It was the only way I could feel like a normal teenage girl, Lisa. Do you have any idea what it's like – seeing how free and happy other girls my age are? Oh, I saw plenty of them on the internet, on Facebook, YouTube, Twitter and everywhere else. They are out at universities or working, always socialising with partners and friends, and I've been stuck in the same house my whole life, basically as a prisoner. I'm nineteen years old, I should be out there living life. When I found the phone and went online, it's the first time I've ever felt normal, or had any friends. I made them because I wanted to look at them and see myself acting like a normal, happy teenager. I also wanted anyone who watched them to see me like that too. That might sound weird, but it's true.' Keep calm, Sophie, I told myself quickly. She's already uncertain about you. All you have to do is keep reassuring her that you are an innocent victim in all this...'

Lisa nodded.

'I can understand all that, Sophie,' she said. 'But the issue my colleagues and I have with your YouTube posts, is that you look so cheerful in them. Not fake happy, but *really* happy. You're singing, dancing, talking about what jobs you want in the future. I mean, let's face it, they don't really scream out "abused girl kept prisoner", do they?'

I stared at her. I knew exactly what she was getting at and it was making a hot anger well up inside me. She didn't understand me. Nobody did. And I had no idea how to accurately portray the complexities of my life to them without it all sounding like an utter shitshow of contrasts and paradoxes. Which is why I'd tried to keep it *simple* in the first place.

'I'm starting to think,' Lisa said, folding her arms and sitting back in her chair. 'That life in the Macreavy house wasn't quite as bad as you've led us to believe, Sophie. I've had a good look round, and some of the food cupboards don't even have locks on. You said they all did. And do you really expect me to believe that every single one of Iris's Facebook photos were faked? And the family picture of all of you on the wall? I mean, come on. How does anyone make four children pretend to be so happy just for a quick snap? What was she doing – poking you with a red-hot iron and commanding you all to smile? I don't think so.'

My fists were clenching under the table, despite the stern talking to that I'd given myself. It was happening again. I'd talked about Iris and Don's abuse and I wasn't being believed. I knew it was a complicated situation, I knew it was hard for people on the outside to understand, but it was *true*. I just hadn't divulged the good, lighter parts of my life. Maybe I shouldn't have kept certain grey areas a secret from the police – in hindsight I should have been totally honest about using Don's old phone, and going on YouTube. But I'd wanted them to *understand* how bad it actually was. And Lisa was totally doubting me now, I could see it in her eyes.

'So that leads me on to my next question, Sophie,' Lisa said. There was something different about her face today, it looked harder, less pretty. The tone of her voice was less warm too. 'If your life wasn't really as bad as you've been making out, and if you've been deceitful with us so far, what else are you hiding? Or lying about? Did you have something to do with any or all of the murders of your family members, Sophie? Is that why you don't seem that bothered by any of their deaths?'

I couldn't talk. My face felt paralysed, my mouth stuck slightly open. Seriously? Was she really and truly asking me this? Anger had now fully swamped the last remnants of fear in me. I felt like hot lava was rising up inside...

I managed to shake my head a little.

'No,' I said. My voice came out as a low, dry rasp. 'How can you possibly ask me this, Lisa?'

Lisa's eyes narrowed a little.

'Because you don't seem to really care about what's happened to your family, Sophie,' she said loudly. 'You've showed next to no interest in the investigation into Iris, Don and Rachel's death – you've barely asked me any questions about it. You didn't seem that bothered when Luke's body was found the other day, in fact you seem more settled, and happier, every time I see you. You're coming across as very cold and uncaring, Sophie. And it's worrying me. And making me wonder why this is.'

I couldn't take my eyes from hers. How was it possible that nice Lisa had morphed into this bitch sitting before me, doubting me? I had an almost irrepressible urge to lean across and slap her back to common sense.

'I've told you the truth about my life,' I said through

clenched teeth. I tried to swallow the hot lava back down, but choked on it instead. 'I had nothing to do with any murders. I know I'm not showing much emotion, and that's puzzling to me too, Lisa. I know it probably seems weird, uncaring. But I can assure you that I'm devastated by the deaths of my family. Overwhelmed, in fact. The only thing I can think is that I'm in shock. I just have this weird numbness inside me. But I'm not a killer. I would never even *wish* anyone dead, even Iris or Don.'

Lisa looked at me, her mouth twisting sideways in a disbelieving way.

'Sure,' she said, standing up. 'If that's the way you want to play it, that's fine, Sophie. But rest assured that my colleagues and I won't rest until we've uncovered the whole truth behind these killings, one way or another.'

Seconds later, I heard the front door click back into place. Lisa was gone.

Fuck. Fuck! What the hell was I supposed to do now?

CHAPTER SEVENTEEN

Okay, so maybe I don't tell the truth the whole, entire time. Not even to myself. But who does? I already know I'm a fairly fucked-up person. I'm coming to terms with the fact that my soul is dark as well as light. Christ, I've been living with Iris for fifteen years – I'm surprised I'm not already completely insane. But being mixed up doesn't make me a murderer, does it?

All right, so I remember most – nearly all – of what happened late Sunday evening, early Monday morning. I just don't want to think about those horrible events. When memories did start filtering back, I knew the police wouldn't understand if I tried to explain, so it seemed easier to convince myself – and them – that I still couldn't remember anything. I really did have a blank about everything in the hospital. I honestly couldn't remember anything to start with; when they told me my parents and Rachel were dead it was a genuine shock. It still is...

Basically, when we were all in the car and Dad was driving through Torquay near the harbour, an almighty argument was raging inside the vehicle. Mum was screaming about how we were all ungrateful bastard children she wished she'd never laid eyes on. How adopting us was her one biggest regret. Dad was yelling about social services, and how I'd single-handedly managed to ruin everyone's lives. He kept asking me how we would manage if they were arrested. Had I thought about that? he said. Rachel was crying – she was getting more hysterical as the voices around her got louder, Jack was yelling back to Dad about how I was right to contact social services, because our parents had made our lives an unbearable hell for years. I was humming loudly, trying to block out all the noise and Don's words. Only Luke was silent. When I looked over at him, I saw him start pounding his forehead with his fists, as though he was in pain. Then in one swift movement he leaned forwards and grabbed Dad's mobile phone from the drink holder near the handbrake. Cue more shouting from Iris and Don, telling him to give it back. But when Dad had to stop because a lorry was blocking the road in front, Luke opened the car door and jumped out, taking the phone with him. Jack leapt out after him, and I also got out. While I was doing so I kept shouting at Rachel:

'Undo your seat belt and come with me,' I kept saying, over and over again. 'Come on, Rachel, this is your chance. Come with me, get out of the car.'

But she seemed frozen, stuck in her seat. Her tear-stained face looked ghostly in the beam of the street light, and she wouldn't talk or move. I knew I couldn't get back in the car because the lorry was moving and I knew Dad would just drive off. I kept yelling at Rachel, but she just couldn't set herself free. The car moved away, jerking, with the back-right passenger door still open. That was the last time I saw anyone in my family, alive or dead. Because when I turned round, Luke and Jack were gone. And that's the truth.

But I can't tell Lisa or any other police officer or detective that I got out of the car with my brothers. They wouldn't understand how I ended back in it again, stabbed and dying along with my parents and sister. And to be honest, I don't understand how that happened either. I just know that I ran into Iris and Don again. I must have. Otherwise why would I have been there on the cliff with them? But if the police are already suspicious of me, there's no way they'd just accept that as a simple explanation. Which is exactly why I'd tried to keep my story straightforward to start with...

CHAPTER EIGHTEEN

I t turns out that my helpful numbness doesn't block out fear. It's now Saturday afternoon, four hours since Lisa left, and frankly I'm going out of my mind. It's clear that Lisa now suspects me, thinks I had something to do with the murders of Iris, Don, Rachel and Luke. But I didn't. However, I know very well that people get blamed for things they didn't do all the time, so I'm continuously shaking at the moment, wondering if there will be a knock at the door – police arriving to arrest me for murder. I remember some stuff I haven't told the police. So what? It doesn't mean I'm a heinous criminal or anything. I don't deserve to be treated like this, I really don't.

Also, I can't get hold of Zach and I so badly need to talk to him. Why does he have to be offline at the time I need to talk to him so badly? I miss him so much it hurts. And he always gives such great advice – I know he'd help me think about what to do. Maybe I could go and stay with him for a while, if he says it's okay? He's already told me he shares an apartment with his brother in the centre of Torquay. I'm sure they wouldn't mind. I'm good at cleaning and I can offer to help – Iris made me do it enough so I'm pretty expert at it now. And he says he really likes me...

Okay. I'm going to pack a bag and just leave. I can't be in this house for one minute longer, I feel like I'm a sitting duck waiting to get shot. I'm getting out of here right now.

CHAPTER NINETEEN

id Adopted Daughter Have Hand in Family's Murders?
The headline in *The Record* jumped out at me as I
walked past the newsagent. Fuck – really? I stepped closer. Yes,
it was about me and my family – I can see the usual photos from
Iris's Facebook page dotted around the article. And more of
Luke in a body bag. And the obligatory photo of me and
Brianna Solotto. That was quick work. I wasn't going to stop
and read it, I don't want to draw attention to myself. Looking at
the title, it suddenly felt like the whole world was out to get me.
But I couldn't help wondering how the paper got this
information – could Lisa be feeding it to them? But why would
she do that? Okay, so at least now I know how deep the
metaphorical pile of shit I'm standing in is – if the media are
presuming I'm guilty of involvement, then it's cavernous.

Okay, it's time to tell Lisa the truth – about everything I
remember. She's a good person at heart, I could see that the first
time I saw her, sitting on the end of my hospital bed. How kind
her eyes were, how warmly she treated me. Then she'll realise
she's got it all wrong, and the police will direct their resources
into finding whoever killed Luke. There's no way I'm getting

out of Iris and Don's enforced prison and going straight into a government one – no way in hell. I'd rather die.

I caught sight of myself in a shop window. The scars on my face were healing well, but I still looked like I'd come off worse in a fight. I found an empty bus stop and perched on a seat, fumbling for my phone. It smelt grimy there, unclean, but I didn't care. Seconds later, I was tapping on Lisa's icon and listening to the ringing tone. It was lucky she saved her number on my device before giving it to me. That was when she was still being nice and helping me...

'Hello?' It was her voice.

'Lisa, hi, it's me, Sophie,' I said. 'Listen, I really need to talk to you. Can I meet you somewhere? It's important. I've got information I really need to tell you.'

There was a pause.

'Sure,' she said, but not in a friendly way. 'I'll meet you outside the McDonald's on the High Street in ten minutes.'

When she arrived, she wasn't smiling.

'Come on,' she said. 'We'll go somewhere private where we can talk.'

A few minutes later, we were sitting on a bench by the skate park. A crushed can of lager lay next to my feet.

'Well?' she said. 'I'm all ears.'

I sighed.

'Thanks so much for giving me a chance to explain,' I said, wondering where to start. Right, Sophie; this is your big chance. Just be as honest as you can – stop withholding things and being so secretive... 'Listen, I know I've been an idiot, and not been very straightforward about everything with you and the detectives. But you don't know what it was like, growing up with Iris and Don. I'm so used to keeping everything a secret, and lying about whatever I do. It was just so important that you all believed my story about the conditions I grew up in. I wanted to fully unmask Iris and Don for who they really were. It makes me sick to my stomach – how so many people seem to think they were wonderful people. Except the church people they fell out with – I know I've told you about them before, you really need to interview all of them, I'm telling you. The life Iris and Don portrayed to the outside world was all a show. It wasn't real. And I can see now, how much it's fucked my head up. But I'm ready to tell you the whole truth now.'

Lisa nodded.

'Go on,' she said.

So I told her about everything – nearly – that I remembered from Sunday evening, about Dad making us get into his car, about the awful arguments, about how Luke snatched the phone and jumped out, followed by Jack and me. I explained that I tried to get Rachel to come out but that she wouldn't move, and that Don and Iris drove off with her still in the car. I told Lisa about the bits of freedom me and the boys had carved out for ourselves, mine being virtual and theirs being to jump out of their bedroom window to meet our uncle Oliver. I really truly was as honest as I could be. Almost…

Lisa listened to everything I said in silence, inclining her head here and there. When I'd finished, she sat quietly for a few seconds.

'Is that really the best you can come up with?' she said eventually.

'What?' I said, feeling like she'd just slapped me. Hang on, what the hell was wrong now?

'Do you seriously expect me to believe the patchwork of lies and half-truths you've just tried to sell me?' Her eyes were hard. 'You must think I was born yesterday, Sophie. Look, let's get real here. We know you were involved with Iris, Don and Rachel's murders, and we suspect you had something to do with Luke's too. And with Jack's disappearance. Your story keeps changing.

To start with, you were happy for us to believe that poor little you were in the car with your parents and sister all along – that you all got attacked by someone terrible together. Then I find out you actually *got out of the car*, well before the stabbing took place. So what's the actual truth here? Why did you end up in the car again? Will you ever be honest about all this or will your story change again?'

I couldn't talk.

'And we know your uncle, Oliver, played a part too,' she went on, before I could find any words. 'Warner told me earlier that she wants you to stop this bullshit and be properly transparent for once. She said that the more you lie, the worse it looks for you. Come on, you're not an idiot, you must be able to see that.'

'I just was transparent about what happened,' I whispered. My hands were shaking. This couldn't be happening. Why didn't she believe me? What more did I need to say? Yes, so I got out of the car when my brothers did. Big deal – it didn't make me a suspect in the murders, it just meant that the truth was more complicated than it first seemed. And yes, I must have met up with my parents and Rachel again, although God knows how, my memories about that bit hadn't come back yet. Perhaps they never would. I could feel my thoughts were slowing down, as if slowly freezing into solid terror. If being honest with Lisa hadn't worked...

'We may not have enough evidence to arrest you today,' Lisa said, standing up and smoothing down her skirt. 'But we will very soon, mark my words. So please don't think for one minute that you've got away with these crimes, Sophie. I'll be coming to see you in an official capacity very soon, to ask you some questions, not as your liaison officer, but as part of the investigation team. So don't even consider going AWOL.' And with that, she walked away.

There's no way Lisa would know that I had temporary plans to pack up and get out of my house. That I felt like a sitting duck there. I don't know what to do about that now, I feel exposed and vulnerable just staying there. But strange things are happening and I need time to think about what to do next. And to be honest, where would I go?

CHAPTER TWENTY

Oh my God. I've well and truly fucked everything up this time, haven't I? If I'd just told the police the truth from the start, none of this would have happened, and Lisa would still be the nice, warm-hearted liaison officer she seemed to be when I first met her. Why can't she see how muddled my mind is? Why are they expecting me to act like a normal person, when my life has been so messed up? Okay, so I told a scrambled version of the truth to them. I omitted some parts and 'forgot' others. I lost my memory to start with, then fragments of that night started coming back in horror-filled bits. But I didn't murder my family! And now Lisa is acting as though I'm a killer. It's not right. Or fair. I've got to do something, or I'll end up going to prison, and I'd rather die than do that. I've only just been given a taste of freedom. And who told the press? It must have been Lisa. But I can't believe she would do something like that.

I've been trying to get hold of Zach all afternoon, but he's still offline. I don't know what to do.

Hang on, what was that crazy thing she said about Uncle Oliver being in cahoots with me over these deaths? Right, I'm finding his number and I'm going to arrange to meet him. Maybe he knows where Jack is. Or perhaps he has more information about the falling out my parents had with the church. If Lisa doesn't believe my words, she can listen to what Oliver has to say instead. He'll put her straight.

CHAPTER TWENTY-ONE

It took half the night to find Uncle Oliver's number. If I still had my dad's old phone it would have been easy – as I knew all his old numbers were still stored on there. However, what actually happened was that I spent hours sifting through my mother's belongings. In her usual cryptic fashion, nothing made sense about the way she stored things. Whereas I've found that Dad tended to keep like with like – books together, diaries together and so on – my mother did not. I found she kept a stash of possessions under her side of the bed, that ranged from a Bible, to a pair of woolly socks, to an old bracelet, and a scarf, a bundle of tangled necklaces, three murder mystery books, an old fleece blanket, a gold rosary, Tolstoy's *War and Peace*, but no address book or list of phone numbers. I eventually found Oliver's number – when I was red-faced, flustered, and sick of searching – in a card he'd written to Mum and Dad six years ago. *Thanks for lending me the money*, his loose writing said. *You've really helped me out. And here's my new number – I've had to get rid of my old phone for various reasons.*

Why would they lend him money? I'd wondered, tidying up the mess I'd made. What had he needed it for? To be honest,

Oliver had never come across as a very responsible adult during the few times I'd seen him. Whereas Iris was icy and controlled, her brother seemed haphazard and he always looked unkempt, like he'd slept in his clothes. He did seem the type who wouldn't be good with looking after himself, so he probably needed some help paying his rent or mortgage or something, I concluded. Strange that they came from the same parents. Also weird that Iris was generous enough to lend him money. Maybe it was only her kids she withheld things from... Mind you, I'm very different from my sister and brothers, we all have – or had – our own quirks, but then we're not blood related, are we?

I tapped Oliver's number into my phone, then held it to my ear. Good, it was ringing.

'Hello?' he said. He sounded tired. It was nearly midday on Sunday.

'Oliver?' I said. 'Hi, it's Sophie Macreavy.'

'Sophie!' I could hear movement and sheets rustling in the background, as though he was sitting up in bed. 'God. How the hell are you? Did you get the card I dropped in for you?'

'Yes, thank you. I'm... I'm not really in a good place at the moment, and I was wondering if you could help me,' I said. I'd never known if Oliver had known or suspected that my parents treated us badly. Maybe his and Iris's parents treated them like that, I didn't know, neither of them had ever said. Or maybe he was just as sucked in by their charade as everyone else. Iris's Facebook page photos looked so authentic, it would take a master of intuition to read between the lines.

'Yeah, yeah, of course.' I could hear Oliver light a cigarette, take a drag, then exhale smoke. 'Poor Iris, Don and Rachel. I still can't believe what happened to them – it's unreal. So unbelievable and tragic. If I can help you in any way, I will, Sophie. What's up – apart from the obvious?'

'I take it you know about Luke?' I said.

'Yeah, I saw the news in the papers,' Oliver said. 'Poor lad; he was a good boy – had a lot of potential. Whoever did this to him needs to be caught and locked up forever.' He sighed deeply. 'This whole situation is awful. So sad.' But not sad enough for you to come round and see me in person, I couldn't help thinking. Or visit me in hospital, even after your sister, brother-in-law and niece were stabbed to death...

I told my uncle what I knew about Luke being found murdered up on Compington Mount, and how I saw his gold Zippo lighter with the dragon motif there on the ground. I also told him about the fact that I seemed to be the police's number one suspect at the moment – how Officer Lisa Denton had decided that my behaviour was so suspicious and unemotional I must have had something to do with all the murders. How she was questioning why I'd left the car that night, and how I'd ended up back in it. But how I was also interrogating myself about that important detail, because it was one I simply couldn't remember.

'And she implicated you too,' I said. 'She told me that she believes you and me were in cahoots somehow, and that you played a part in my family's demise.'

'She *what?*' Oliver's voice was louder now. Harder, annoyed. 'That's bloody ridiculous. She certainly hasn't said anything to me, I don't even know which police officer you're talking about. The only ones I met were the two that came to tell me about Iris, Don and Rachel. And they were both men.'

'So she hasn't contacted you at all?' I said, my forehead wrinkling. 'Okay, that's weird, after what she was saying. But maybe she was just trying to scare me by making things up about you. Listen, Oliver, if I give you her number can you call her and tell her that you and I had nothing to do with killing them? That we haven't planned anything together? I'm freaking out that I'll end up in prison for something I didn't do, and I know I won't be able to handle it if that does happen.' My hand holding the phone was shaking now. The thought of losing my freedom again literally made me want to vomit. I'd been through so much already in my short nineteen years of life, I just wanted an easier ride now. And yes, to find out who was behind the murders and where the hell Jack was. But mainly, I wanted to be free – I realised that now.

'Ah,' Oliver said, breathing out. 'Er, the thing is, Sophie – me and the police don't have the best relationship. Historically.'

'What do you mean?' I said.

'It's just that when I was younger, you know, a stupid teenager' – Oliver was speaking slowly, obviously choosing his words carefully – 'I did some silly things I shouldn't have. And I did spend a few nights in police cells then.'

'Are you kidding?' This time *my* voice was getting louder. Suddenly I was wondering if my uncle *could* be involved in all the deaths after all. Why was he acting so strangely? Surely he would jump at the chance to clear his niece's name? He was certainly very different from his seemingly perfect law-abiding sister. There was so much I didn't know about him. 'What kind of things?'

'Oh nothing serious,' Oliver said. 'Just smoking pot, getting too drunk, maybe being involved with the odd fight, stuff like that.'

'Oh my God.' I sat down on the sofa.

'So the thing is,' he went on. 'It's probably best if I *don't* contact the police, Sophie. I know that sounds harsh, and it's not what you want to hear, but I don't think they'd believe me if I did try and defend your good name. I've spent a long time avoiding them, and I just don't think it would be a good idea to call attention to myself again. But if you need anything else, like food, a lift somewhere, help organising the funerals, then I'm your man, just let me know and I'll be over in a shot to help.'

There was a pause. 'Look,' he said. 'If you ask me, it's that church lot you and the police should be looking at in connection with this. I've already told the coppers that, not that they listened. Iris and Don never told me very much about what happened, but I do know that my sister was genuinely scared after they withdrew from the church. One night she told me she was convinced that certain people from it were after her. I could tell from her face how worried she was.'

Church members? Okay, I had to look into this – tell the police they should be concentrating on the God squad instead of me. Goodness knows why they hadn't said more about it so far. If I flagged it up with Lisa and the detectives then hopefully they'd finally take this lead more seriously. And funerals? Fuck, I hadn't even thought about those. Mind you, one or other of the detectives had told me the bodies would be retained until they had finished their investigation...

'Fine,' I said, slumping. 'Don't worry about it, Oliver. Thanks for the tip about the church.' I rang off before he had a chance to say goodbye, then threw the phone down next to me. Now what? My uncle clearly had no intention of helping. And it was weird that he'd said Lisa had never even contacted him. She'd sounded so sure he was involved. But maybe she was bluffing, just trying to scare me? Yep, that was probably her tactic. But even so, a nagging feeling tugged at the thoughts at the very back of my head. My thoughts were shifting suddenly. Morphing into a different shape, a new order. She'd gone from nice to tough so quickly, it had felt weird, not right. And she wasn't giving me a chance to explain why I'd made the YouTube videos, and why I hadn't been honest about them. From what I'd seen on her Facebook page, she and her boyfriend were well-respected police officers – so she must be good at her job. She must know what she's doing, and have a good reason for treating me like this. But something felt wrong. I'd gone from being treated as the victim to being treated as a suspect in a matter of a few days. Lisa must be getting information about me from somewhere or someone – but who? And had she really fed her beliefs to the paper? Surely that would be unprofessional. But if she hadn't done it, then someone else was out to get me. Someone – perhaps – who had killed Luke, and potentially harmed Jack.

I looked down at my hands and realised they were shaking. The reality hit me: not only was I a suspect in the police's eyes, but my life was in danger – real danger. What if I was next on some psychopath's list? How had I not realised this before? I'd been too worried about what I was telling the police. The actual reality of the threat that hung over me hadn't been something I'd been focusing on.

My mind started racing. My opinion of Oliver had gone further down since talking to him – maybe he was involved somehow? Maybe he was trying to deliberately mislead me by pointing a finger at members of their church? Or what if what he said was true? Did he know more than he was telling me? I needed to find out more about the people in the church who'd fallen out with my parents. But hang on, in the card I'd found from my uncle to Mum and Dad he'd talked about them lending him money, hadn't he? Well, maybe he was hard up for cash again and decided to finish them off so he could benefit from their wills. Oh God, my mind was all over the place, I didn't know what to think. Everyone around me suddenly seemed dangerous. Unreliable. Untrustworthy. My only sibling still possibly alive was Jack – I had no idea where he'd gone or who he could be with. I hoped he was still alive, but what if he'd had something to do with all this and Luke's murder? The police seemed to find his past behaviour suspicious. He'd always had an anger problem, what if he'd snapped and organised all this as a way to get free from our family? Or maybe Mum or Dad had been involved with some shady people who'd done this for some reason or other? Even Luke could have got to know people without me realising – when he jumped out of the window at nights. It suddenly dawned on me how little I'd known about the people I'd grown up with for years. We'd been kept so apart emotionally by Iris, we were like isolated islands living close together. But then, none of them had known I'd nicked Dad's old phone and gone on social media, had they? Maybe we all had secrets from each other, and one of those secrets had been dark enough to cause all this tragedy. I mean, I know it wasn't me who caused any of the deaths. And I'm trying to be completely honest with Lisa about everything now. But I don't know if I'll ever be able to fully do that... not with the darkness that's been bred inside me by Iris like a curse... Some things are better left unsaid...

CHAPTER TWENTY-TWO

I went back upstairs and pulled out all of Mum and Dad's old diaries that I could find. I tried not to breathe through my nose, I didn't want to get a hint of Iris's perfume again. I now knew I needed to know more about what led to them leaving the local church, maybe try and find some members of it and ask them about what happened, and give their names to the police. I was now doubly motivated: I needed to clear my name and save my life. Something horrific was afoot that I didn't understand, I felt that in my bones, and I didn't for one minute believe that Jack could be behind it. There had to be another explanation.

This time it didn't take long to find the information I needed to start my search. My mother's diaries – I could only find two of hers – were full of wispy, fragmented comments that didn't make much sense. But Don – clearly the more organised of the partnership – had neat lists of church contacts in the back of one of his oldest diaries. Seven had red stars next to them. Why would that be? I had no idea, but these people seemed like the perfect ones to start with. My father had singled them out for a reason, and I intended to find out why.

I started with the first red-starred name – Peter Ainsworth. I typed his number into my phone, pressed the call button, and waited.

'Hello?' It was a man's gruff voice.

'Hi, Peter?' I said. 'This is Sophie Macreavy. I'm sorry to bother you, but I was wondering if you could help me. I'm looking for information connected to my parents?'

'Macreavy?' he repeated.

'Yes,' I said. 'Iris and Don were my parents.'

The line went dead. He'd hung up. What? How strange. I tried the next red-starred name in the list – Mrs Hattie Wright.

'Hattie Wright speaking?' an elderly lady's voice answered. I repeated my introduction to her, hoping she wouldn't hang up.

'There's nothing I want to talk to you about,' the woman said, her tone now severe. 'Don't call this number again. I'm warning you...'

Right, this was getting strange. Why wouldn't these people talk to me? What could possibly have happened all those years ago? I silently cursed Iris and Don for never telling us anything about their lives. Why did they always have to be so secretive? What on earth did they have to hide that could be this bad?

I tried three more numbers, but not one of them answered. I hoped Peter and Hattie weren't tipping the others off about me phoning now, telling them not to answer if an unknown number called them.

Feeling deflated and despondent, I called number six of the red-starred names – Maurice Jenkins. A woman answered, and I explained I'd like to speak to Maurice.

'He died two years ago,' she said. Dead end there then. Literally.

I tried my last hope, the seventh red-starred name – Cora Unwin. She actually answered, and I repeated my introduction once more.

'Look,' she said. 'Hattie just texted me, saying you'd

probably ring. I don't know how you got our numbers, but just leave it, okay? What happened is done and dusted. I've read the papers, I know your poor parents are dead. So it's time to leave the past well behind, where it belongs. You better listen to what I'm saying, dear, or I can assure you things will get very bad for you.'

She hung up.

I stood there, stunned. Did Cora Unwin just threaten me? It was such an incongruous thing to have happened, I couldn't quite believe it. Cora, clearly an older lady with a well-spoken voice, had just tried to intimidate me. It was unreal. What the actual hell?

I was going to pass all these names on to the police as soon as I could. But now I needed a friend to talk to. I felt so tired inside, so sick of all of this crap. I needed Zach. I needed him to tell me everything would be okay. I'd initiated this for him, after all. He'd been the one who told me to lie to Iris and Don about the social services in the first place...

CHAPTER TWENTY-THREE

I logged on to Facebook again; I wanted to see if Zach had read my messages, or even better, sent one back. I really, desperately hoped he had. He was now the only person in my life that I could rely on. But before I even had a chance to press on the message icon, I saw a news headline from *Torquay Live* flash up on my feed:

Teenage boys admit to hiding 'missing' Jack Macreavy.

Hang on... What the actual fuck? Why hadn't the police let me know? Surely Jack could now exonerate me from any involvement? My heart rate immediately increased tenfold and I read on.

Owen Johnson and Brett Ryan from Melville Road have admitted hiding seventeen-year-old Jack Macreavy in their house since Sunday evening. Today Johnson posted this announcement on his Twitter page: 'Stop searching for Jack everyone, he's with me and Brett. He doesn't want to be found. Leave him alone.' Police say they are investigating Johnson's claims.

Jack was alive! Oh, this was fantastic news. I sat thinking for a few minutes. If Jack was safe and well, then all I had to do was head up to Melville Road and find him. He'd help clear my name, I knew he would. I could feel hope flooding back into my brain in waves, and it felt intoxicating.

My phone burst into life. I answered it.

'Sophie?' It was a woman's voice.

'Yes?'

'This is Detective Warner. I have some news and I wanted you to be the first to know. Some irresponsible tabloid printed a story about Jack being alive and well with some boys from Melville Road today. We've looked into it and I'm afraid it's not true. The boys were just messing around, apparently they thought it would be funny to pretend they were looking after Jack, God knows why. We pulled them in for questioning and they admitted to making the whole thing up as a hoax. I'm very sorry to tell you this, and I wanted you to know in case you read about it in the media.'

I exhaled, my spirits plummeting once again.

'Thanks,' I said. 'I'd just read the article. I was so happy that Jack was alive.'

'He may still be,' Detective Warner said. 'Let's hope for the best. We are doing everything we can to find him.'

I rang off and a single tear rolled down my cheek. Talk about a high followed by a low. I was back to square one. At least she hadn't threatened or accused me like Lisa had. Which on second thoughts, was somewhat strange...

CHAPTER TWENTY-FOUR

Wanting – needing – something more concrete to unfold about who the fuck was responsible for this carnage, I reached over to the pile of diaries belonging to Don and Iris, still in a stack on the table. The angry lava was back. My blood felt hot as it pumped round my body. Why should I have to investigate this? Why should I have to work to clear my name, and prove who was really guilty in all of this? It was so unfair, so desperately wrong. I pulled the top one off, slammed it on the table and flicked it open. It was Iris's, and from the date on the front it was one she'd used thirteen years ago.

I read her loopy writing.

Life's too hard sometimes.

I flicked over.

I'm waiting for something to change but it never does.

I flicked further. The whole thing seemed to be full of these vague, discouraged statements. While they might tell me a lot about Iris's state of mind, they didn't shed any light on the difficulties she and my dad were having with the church at that time, or with anything else.

As I carried on looking through it, a bigger block of her writing caught my eye. It stood out from the rest, because usually she just wrote one or two sentences per page and left it at that. This paragraph was longer, more in-depth.

They're out to get me, Hattie made that quite clear when I ran into her at the post office today. The way she stared at me, honestly, if looks could kill... They hate me now. I'm so scared. After everything I've done for them over all these years. Ungrateful wretches. And all of it's a mistake, a huge misunderstanding. At least, that's the message I need to get across. But I can't go there anymore. From now on, we're a nuclear family at home. We don't need the outside world; it's nothing but trouble.

Scared? Why would she be scared of Hattie? I'd only spoken to the old lady for a few seconds, but she'd sounded as scary as a newborn puppy on the phone. What the hell happened all those years ago? What misunderstanding was she talking about?

I found Don's diary again, and copied Hattie's address out on to the back of an envelope and put it in my pocket. A face-to-face call would be my next move with these church people – starting with Hattie, as she was the one my mother had specifically mentioned. If I was standing on her doorstep, the old lady would have to speak to me, surely? Especially if I explained how important this all was. If Hattie and friends had no vendetta against my family, especially no marked interest in ending the life of my siblings, then she would have no reason to hide anything. She should be able to tell me the truth. I let out a growl and pulled at my hair until it hurt. This was all beyond frustrating. I needed answers, but all I was finding were more questions...

Zach would know what to do. He always kept me sane in the past when I was upset or anxious. I needed to speak to him so badly. But why had he been offline for so long? I pulled out my phone...

CHAPTER TWENTY-FIVE

Zach had disappeared from Facebook, and for some reason it was bothering me more than any of the other tragedies swirling around me. It was so unlike him; he'd been there for me for months. He was supposed to be my friend, my support. I'd started feeling things for him that I hadn't for anyone else in the world. And it was him who'd suggested I lie and tell Iris and Don that social services were after them. And now he thought it was a good idea to just vanish, when I needed him the most? That hurt, it really did. Hot tears fell down my cheeks and I slapped them away, then slammed my fists on the table. This was the last straw. I'd felt buoyant when Zach was supporting me; his care had lifted me up – become almost more important than anything else, even the ties I felt to my siblings. I'd got to the point where I felt I would do almost anything he suggested, go through with whatever he wanted me to if only it meant we could still be friends, keep talking, maybe meet up one day, and then... I'd hoped that more would happen...

It was half three on Sunday afternoon, and I didn't know what to do, where to go, or who – if anyone – to turn to for help. It was the most desolate I'd felt since leaving the hospital. The false news about Jack being with the boys in Melville Road had really shaken me. Zach's apparent abandonment had nearly killed me. I felt the most alone I ever had in my life, and that was saying something. For the thousandth time, an image of me in a jail cell flashed through my mind.

Right, that's enough. I heaved myself out of the sofa and shook my head. I was an independent person now – and I had to think like one. No one else was going to do that for me. Most of my family was dead, Jack was still missing, Oliver was useless, Lisa had turned on me, and Zach had disappeared from Facebook. The only person who was going to help me now, was me. So I was going to stop sitting around feeling sorry for myself and do some investigating of my own, I decided. There was no fucking way in hell that I intended to be in literal or metaphorical chains ever again.

I was, I now knew, going to properly find out what the hell had happened – not only to my family and Luke – but to Jack too. By myself. Because it seemed that I couldn't rely on anyone else in the world. And I'm sad to say it wasn't because of grief for the others, but more for my own selfish purposes; I needed to make sure Lisa and the other police knew the truth and stopped suspecting me. I needed to guarantee my personal freedom. I knew this was selfish but I didn't care.

And the first thing I was going to do was to look for Jack. Because if he was still alive, I bet my life that he knew a lot about what the fuck had happened to Luke and the rest of the family...

CHAPTER TWENTY-SIX

It was about four o'clock in the afternoon when I closed the front door behind me and headed for Compington Mount. I was going on foot, partly because I didn't feel comfortable getting a taxi on my own, and partly because I wanted to remain anonymous and undetected. A deep mistrust for society had overtaken me. I'd always imagined that I'd have a better life once I was free from Iris and Don, but I'd been wrong. It seemed that there were lots of other corrupt people and forces in the world – like the police – who wanted to take my life and freedom away again. And I just couldn't allow that to happen. Zach's disappearance had cut through me, sickened me, destroyed the uplifted feeling that had been running parallel to the awfulness of the murders. Bad as it may sound, I'd felt a sense of emancipation since I was told that Iris and Don were dead. And this, coupled with my growing relationship with Zach had elevated me inside. But now, since his radio silence, I just felt hardened. Pissed off. Zach had given me hope. His desertion had taken it away. I needed to find my own reasons to exist, to carry on. I needed to stoke up the fight in me...

I'd found an old dark-green rucksack at the bottom of the boys' cupboard – among other odds and ends – and filled it with necessary things: a torch, sandwiches, a bottle of water, an extra jumper and a large kitchen knife. The knife was a last-minute addition, but as my own safety was my primary concern now, I figured it may come in handy. Fuck everybody else.

The autumn light was fading as I turned left out of the gate. The air was cold, a chill wind making me shiver. It felt daunting, but kind of rousing, to be setting off on my first ever mission alone. I felt exposed and vulnerable, yet at liberty and independent – all at the same time. I felt more angry, but stronger, with each step. A strange mixture of sensations that had my adrenaline pumping at high levels. I didn't pass many people as I consulted Google Maps. I ignored those that I did, turning down road after road, with the ground level getting noticeably higher with each stretch.

The landscape of Torquay – as I know from my days studying the guide book – is very dramatic and sloping, which is probably due to the Sticklepath fault line that runs through it. The town and harbour are at low levels, whereas many houses and roads wind upwards towards higher ground, including the incline of Compington Mount. I'm not going to pretend that my heart didn't beat faster, and that I didn't take a good few looks behind me as I walked away from the residential roads and on to the more deserted highway, Cliff Heights, that turned off the main road. I may have been angry but I was never unaware of the danger I'd now realised I was in. Google Maps was telling me that if I kept walking up, I'd eventually get to a small turning on my left that would lead me into the wilderness of the mount. The pavement had disappeared, so I balanced on the grass verge and hoped that the occasional cars zooming past would miss me. Half of me didn't really care all that much if one hit me and killed me, but the strong bit of me – the bit that was growing – did care. It felt that I had a right to exist, and that I should carry on doing so for as long as possible. Come on, Sophie, tap into what fight remains in you...

By the time I saw the turning to my left, darkness had descended, and my calf muscles – still unused to walking for any amount of time – were aching badly. Was this where Lisa had parked her car, the time she'd taken me here to see Luke in his body bag? I thought so, but couldn't be sure. The pale moon shone in the sky above, which gave everything around me a ghostly feel. Then a looming cloud cut out a section of its light. Damn it. I crossed the road and turned my torch on, pausing for a minute to catch my breath, and to summon up the energy to walk into the blackness of the wooded mount. Never in a million years did I ever think I'd be doing something like this – alone – or with anyone else for that matter. But, Sophie, I gave myself a pep talk, you are all you have left now. You have to clear your name, and you need to find Jack in order to start doing that. You do have a right to live, you deserve to have a good life, after all you've been through. Get it together.

Fine, I replied internally. Then let's go. Stop being scared and get on with it.

Lunging forward between two trees, I shone the torchlight in front of me, and stepped over a mess of fallen branches. There, I was in. A whoosh of wet, decaying vegetation reached my nose. Minutes later, I was fully immersed in an eerie world of tree trunks, dead leaves and brambles, all coming and going in front of me as my yellow electric light swung to and fro in the enveloping darkness. I could see no beginning and no end to the claustrophobic scrub I was surrounded by. I now knew that the moonlight barely got a chance to shine through the wilderness on the mount; even though the leaves had started falling the conifers and general foliage were thick enough to block it out. Or perhaps the clouds had now fully obscured its light. Despite my best efforts at retaining my angry compulsion to find my brother, an edge of apprehension, which flowed into fear, entered my veins. Its potency increased with each step.

Fuck. I looked around. I had no idea where I was. I had no choice but to keep going. I tried really hard to keep Jack's face in my mind's eye; *he* was why I was doing this. I had to find him, no matter what. He would tell the police who attacked Luke, I know he would. But thoughts that murderers and/or rapists were hiding behind each tree, waiting to attack me, kept flashing through my mind. Time started to become fluid; I had no idea how long I'd been walking – and tripping – over the mount's surface. It seemed like hours, but when I checked my phone I saw that only twenty-six minutes had passed since I'd left the main road.

On and on I went, my legs tired now, my heartbeat racing. I kept scanning the ground in front of me with the torchlight, feeling desperate, looking for something identifiable that told me I was near the place where Luke was found. It didn't take Lisa and I this amount of time to walk from the road to where he was lying; so I must either be lost, or I was missing vital clues about where the right spot was. Maybe I'd end up alone and walking on Compington Mount forever; no one knew where I was so no one could rescue me.

Then I saw it to my right in the torchlight, the swimming pool of blackness beyond what looked like the edge of a cliff. I recognised the tree stump and the two strangely intertwined trunks. I remembered the journalists standing near them. I ran over and shone my torch downwards; sure enough, I was standing on the edge of the same crevice that all the media people had been on when Lisa and I arrived to see Luke's body. I thought it was the same place, because below me there was still a bit of a mess. Obviously there was no body and no police, but there was a long dent in the leaves where Luke had lain, and the area still looked disturbed and unkempt.

I jumped down to investigate. The remains of a small fire were left over to one side, and I saw two cigarette butts when I kicked a pile of leaves with my foot. Yes, this was the right spot, I was sure of it now. I combed the ground as closely as I could, concentration now overtaking terror. The police had evidently taken as many of the rubbish items as they could; there were no more cans or packets around, and the Zippo lighter had gone too. But what if they'd missed something, something that would help me? I widened my search area and examined a further ten metre radius from where Luke had lain. It was difficult in the dark, my arm was hurting from holding the torch out and I kept going back over places in case I'd missed something.

Ah, what was that half under a log? I bent down and looked. Oh my God. It was Jack's glasses. About a year ago he'd wrapped Sellotape around one of the arms after he'd dropped and damaged them. Iris and Don refused to buy him a new pair; they resented any penny they had to spend on us. I also recognised the scratched tortoiseshell frames; these spectacles were definitely my brother's. I reached forward and carefully dislodged them and brought them towards me. How had the police missed such a vital clue? And what did it mean, that they were here and not on Jack's face? Had someone planted them here after Luke's body was taken away? Jack would need these, he was as blind as a bat without them. He wore them from the moment he woke up to the minute he went to bed. He wouldn't be without them by choice. Fuck, did this mean something had happened to him too? Yes, it must.

I shone the torch on them, studying them closely. There was a crack in one lens, and the other arm – which had been undamaged the last time I'd seen my brother wearing them –

was now hanging off at an angle. Either he'd dropped them, or they'd come off due to some sort of force, I thought. And if Jack had dropped them himself, he wouldn't have left the area until he'd found them again, I knew that. They were a part of him that he just couldn't do without. This was proof, in my eyes, that he'd been attacked too. I *knew* he hadn't had anything to do with the murders. But where was he now?

With terror tinged with the now familiar anger ramping back up inside me, I stood up and shone the torch around again. If the police had missed these, what else was still here?

Then I stopped, staying rigidly still, barely daring to breathe.

It was the crackle of a twig breaking that had made me freeze. I listened, still not breathing. It had sounded like a footstep. Shit and fuck. Or had it been a branch falling? No, it had been too crunchy. I waited.

There was another crack, then another. Someone was walking towards me in the darkness. I swung the torchlight around, but could only see ghostly trees and undergrowth. I wanted to breathe now, but I couldn't. I didn't want to die. Not now, not here. Stupid girl, why had I come here by myself? In one swift movement, I swung my rucksack off my back and undid the clasp. My hand trembling, I reached in for the kitchen knife and held it in front of me. Would this be how I died? On Compington Mount, like Luke?

'Sophie?' A man's voice I recognised filled the air. Oliver.

'Yes?' I said, still holding the knife out. I now trusted no one, not even my uncle. What the fuck was he doing up here? Was he a liar? A murderer?

'Thank God it's you,' Oliver said, his voice getting closer. 'I don't know why you're here – I can't even begin to guess – but I'm very glad to see you.' I could make him out now, a shadowy figure coming towards me.

'What the fuck are you doing up here?' My voice came out harsh. I didn't trust him one bit.

'I'll explain that soon, but first you need to come with me,' Oliver said. 'Put that knife down, please, Sophie. I mean you no harm. You have to listen to me. I've found Jack.'

CHAPTER TWENTY-SEVEN

I stared at the man now standing beside me. I saw that he was holding a thick stick in his lowered hand.

'You've found Jack?' I repeated, my mind instantly a whirl.

'Yes,' Oliver said. 'He's badly injured, covered in blood, and unconscious. He's barely alive, but he's still taking very shallow breaths. If we phone the paramedics now there may still be a chance for him. Do you have a phone with you?'

I nodded.

'Yes,' I said. 'Show me where he is.'

By the time we got to my brother, I'd put the knife away and was holding my phone. As I gazed down at my poor brother's bloodied face, illuminated by Oliver's torch, I was already punching in the nines. Nausea was sitting high in my throat, my hands shaking with every movement.

Ten minutes later, Compington Mount was swarming with emergency workers of all types. Their lights illuminated everything; it was no longer scary on the mount, it had suddenly morphed into a sterile recovery scene. A helicopter landed somewhere nearby – probably the road – and soon paramedics had Jack on a stretcher and were walking out of the wood with him. Detectives Warner and Pierce had also arrived, and were standing either side of me. It hadn't escaped my notice that at some point – amid all the chaos – my uncle Oliver had disappeared. I couldn't see him anywhere. But I wasn't going to tell the police about him being there – not yet. I had my own reasons for that...

'What were you doing up on Compington Mount, Sophie?' Detective Pierce said, his voice low and level.

I sighed.

'I wanted to find Jack,' I said. As the words left my lips I knew they sounded lame. Unbelievable.

'And what a coincidence. You did,' Detective Warner said, turning towards me. 'I think it's about time you came down to the station for a chat, Sophie, don't you?'

CHAPTER TWENTY-EIGHT

I've always hated bright overhead lights. They are so stark and unforgiving. So sitting under one opposite Detective Warner and Detective Pierce in an interview room wasn't helping my mood.

'We know what you've told Lisa so far, Sophie,' Detective Warner was saying. 'About what happened on Sunday evening, how your father made you all get into his car, and how you and the boys got out when an opportunity arose. But why don't you tell us everything you remember about that evening. Don't leave anything out. Start from the beginning. Take your time.'

So I did. I told them exactly what I'd said to Lisa: the truth. I went into as much detail as possible. They sat quiet and unsmiling before me as I talked, occasionally nodding or making notes.

'Look, I know I'm your number one suspect,' I said, leaning forward and resting my chin on my hands. 'And I have to tell you I think that's ridiculous. I can't believe you would think that, especially after everything I've been through. After you saw me with your own eyes in the hospital, after everything I told you about Iris and Don. I mean, look at me. I'm skin and bone. I don't have the muscle to do harm to anyone, even if I wanted to. And I care – cared – about my siblings very much. None of them deserved what happened to them.' I could feel wetness soaking my eyes.

Detective Warner turned to her colleague and raised her eyebrows.

'Number one suspect?' she said. There was a smile playing on the edge of her lips. 'That's a bit dramatic isn't it, Sophie? No, I can tell you that you are not our main suspect. At this point you are a person of interest to us, along with everyone who knew your family members. We are simply trying to unravel this mysterious mess and get to the truth. We need to know how it was that – coincidentally – you were there on Compington Mount this evening, and somehow managed to find your badly injured brother. We know he wasn't there before, our search teams have combed the whole mount several times. There may be a very good reason why you were there, we just need you to explain it to us.'

'But Lisa said...' I started.

'Yes?' Detective Pierce was staring right at me.

I exhaled.

'The way Lisa was talking to me, it sounded like you'd all pretty much made up your minds that I'm responsible for all the murders,' I said, suddenly feeling very tired. 'Even before today.'

'That's not correct,' Detective Warner said, shaking her head. 'And I'm sure Lisa never said those exact words to you, did she? She was probably trying to get more of the truth out of you, Sophie, and trying different strategies. I mean, you haven't exactly been very forthcoming with it so far, would you agree? When I came to see you in the hospital you said you couldn't remember anything about Sunday evening, then a few days later you tell Lisa you can remember everything. It doesn't take a genius to work out why that looks slightly suspicious, does it?

Can you see that your story keeps changing, and how inconsistent that looks to us?'

I shook my head. I was trying to remember Lisa's precise words to me, but as usual these days my mind was a total mess. I knew she'd implicated me in the crimes, threatened me in fact. But now things in my head were a blur and I couldn't recall her precise words. Fuck it.

'But Lisa...' I stopped again. 'She definitely said you all knew it was me who was behind all the killings.' My head was aching now.

'Was it you?' Detective Pierce said.

'No.' My voice was loud now.

'Do you think all the stress of this week is making you a bit paranoid, Sophie?' Detective Warner leaned forwards. 'Lisa Denton is a professional. She's good at her job. There's no way she'd accuse you of something outright if we didn't have the evidence – which we don't. Maybe you need to speak to a psychologist?'

I put my head in my hands. Someone was going mad and I was afraid it was me.

'Why did you go up Compington Mount this evening, Sophie?' Detective Pierce said. 'How did you know you were going to find Jack?' He was gazing right at me.

'I didn't know,' I said through clenched teeth, looking right back at him. 'I was hoping I'd find a clue or something about what happened to him. I didn't know I'd actually find my brother. I'm glad I found him. Hopefully he'll get better and he can help me clear my name. He knows the truth, he'll remember who attacked him. And it wasn't me. You're just like Lisa. You're treating me as a suspect, no matter what you say. That's why I went up there by myself. No one else is helping me, so I have to do all this on my own.'

Detective Pierce crossed his arms and sat back in his chair, still looking at me.

'All we are doing, Sophie,' Detective Warner said, 'is trying to understand *you* at this point. And all the different things you've done and said. You have to admit you aren't exactly making things easy for yourself. Look, we wanted to show you the CCTV we've recovered of the night in question. I think you'll find it quite interesting, and it may help to jog your memory about a few things.'

Seconds later we were all staring at a grainy video. It looked like it was filmed from high up somewhere, maybe from above a shop. I watched my father's blue SUV jerk to a halt behind a truck. Before the car had finished moving the back door opened and Luke tumbled out, followed closely by me and Jack. It was weird seeing my brothers so alive and healthy. I wished they were still like that; they didn't deserve whatever it was that happened to them. Poor boys. I was riveted now, unblinking, as I saw me getting out of the car, then standing by it. There was no sound on the video, but I could see my mouth open and close, my arms waving around, sometimes reaching back into the vehicle. I knew what I was doing – I was shouting at Rachel, trying to convince her to leave with us. But then my attention was drawn to something else on the video. Jack and Luke stood a few metres behind me; they were talking in what looked like an urgent way. Then Luke saw something that wasn't on camera, and he made Jack turn and look at whatever it was. Just for a second, I saw a woman in the corner of the screen – she seemed to be talking to someone off camera. I couldn't see her face, but she had long, light-coloured wavy hair and was dressed in a cheap kind of way, with tiny shorts, a shiny jacket and high heels. Who the hell was that, and why did Jack and Luke seem to recognise either her or the person she was talking to? As I went on shouting at Rachel in the car, oblivious to what was going on behind me, I saw the woman beckon to Luke and Jack. They looked towards me, then walked to her – and all three of them disappeared off the video. I saw myself drag my hands through my hair as the truck moved off and Dad's SUV jerked into life, driving off with the passenger door still hanging open. Then his car disappeared from the screen too.

Detective Pierce turned the screen off, and looked at me again.

'So,' he said. 'We know you are telling the truth about what you remember from Monday night, Sophie. Your story about how you, Jack and Luke exited the car matches the CCTV recording exactly, which is great. It means you are being honest about that bit. It proves we can trust some of the things you are saying. Slowly, the real truth is emerging. But now we also have it confirmed that you left the car, too, at that time – which presents a rather gaping inconsistency with what we first believed; that you were with your parents the whole time from leaving home to being attacked. As I'm sure you understand, we now need to get to the bottom of what happened to you during the intervening time. Where did you go at that point, after you'd exited the vehicle? How did you end up back in the family car later on? What happened, Sophie? Do you actually remember who stabbed your mother, father, sister and yourself?'

I stared at him for a moment, then shook my head.

'I don't remember,' I said slowly. 'I have no idea. Honestly. I must have met up with them again – I mean, I obviously did because that's where I was found – but the in-between bits are still all a blank in my mind. Don probably came back and my parents must have forced me to get back into the car. I'm telling the truth, Detective, you have to believe me.'

Detective Pierce twisted his mouth sideways, then nodded.

'Sure,' he said. 'Hopefully your memory will come back soon, and you'll be able to tell us more. Also, another thing we need to know now is the identity of the woman your brothers are talking to?'

'I don't know that either,' I said. 'As you can see from the film, I didn't see the woman who was beckoning to my brothers. All that happened behind me when my full attention was focused on trying to get Rachel to get out of the car. I knew Iris and Don were beyond mad that night, and I was seriously concerned for her safety, I was really worried about what would happen when they all drove off again. I thought – presumed – that my brothers were still standing behind me all the time I was talking to Rachel. I had absolutely no idea that they'd gone anywhere until Dad drove off and I turned around. It honestly shocked me that they disappeared as much as it surprised you. And that's the truth. Watch more of the video and you'll see what happened. When I turned around and looked, I couldn't spot them anywhere. You'll understand.'

'We have watched more – we've watched the whole thing many times,' Detective Warner said, shifting position. 'And yes, we see you turn around, and then also exit in roughly the same direction as your brothers did. Which leads us to believe you must have known where they'd gone, and with whom. Your father's car stopped in the red-light district, frequented by prostitutes. We've all just watched that happen on the CCTV video. Were Luke or Jack in the habit of going there? Did you all cause something to happen in the car to stop it at that point? Perhaps you had all prearranged to meet someone there? It's a possibility as we now know you all had more freedom than you initially let on. Perhaps you all had a wider social network than you first led us to believe.'

I reached up and tugged at clumps of my hair.

'I. Do. Not. Know. Where. They. Went,' I said slowly and loudly. 'I have no idea if they ever visited prostitutes but I highly doubt it. Just because they jumped out of the window to smoke with my uncle Oliver occasionally, and I stole my dad's old phone so I could have a lifeline to the outside world, just because we helped ourselves to a tiny bit of freedom, doesn't mean we led a normal life. We didn't, we could hardly do anything, Iris made sure of that. It was a living hell in that house, whichever way you look at it. And it doesn't matter how many times you ask me, my answer will still be the same, because it's the truth. I don't know who the woman was. I don't know if or how my brothers might have known her. I don't know where they went afterwards, and I certainly wasn't with them. And I have no idea what happened in between me leaving the car and ending up stabbed with my parents and Rachel. I can remember walking off by myself that night, and that's it. Blank after that.'

Both detectives stared at me, their facial expressions bland. Detective Pierce picked up a pen and tapped it on the table.

'Okay, Sophie,' he said after a moment or two. 'Perhaps we all need to take a short break. We can carry on our interview after that.'

I threw my head back and let out a strange roar. I used to do that when Iris locked me in my room for hours. It was some guttural reaction to being cornered.

I sat up and slammed my hands down on the table.

'Actually, if I'm not a suspect, am I free to go?' I said.

Detective Pierce nodded.

'Absolutely,' he said.

'Then I'm leaving,' I said. I stood up.

CHAPTER TWENTY-NINE

My thoughts were racing as I headed off into the night. Anger, fear, confusion, exasperation and a desperate need for everything to be okay jostled for pride of place in my emotions. I felt like every police officer I came in contact with was screwing with my head. Why were those two pretending that I wasn't their main suspect? Now that I was away from them, Lisa's exact words were coming back to me: *'Please don't think for one minute that you've got away with these crimes, Sophie'*. She had directly stated her beliefs to me, throwing my words right back into my face, whereas the other two detectives had been annoyingly nuanced and subtle, refusing to commit to the fact that they were suspicious of me. Although they clearly were. Were they allowed to act like that? In such a fucked up, bewildering way? Probably, I thought, rounding a corner. Bastards.

I reached into my jacket pocket and pulled out my phone. I googled the place I knew they'd taken Jack to – Torbay Hospital – and found the phone number. Seconds later I'd reached the switchboard.

'Hello?' I said, when someone answered. 'Please can you

put me through to Jack Macreavy's ward? He's my brother. He was brought in today, very badly injured. I need to find out how he is.'

Soon, a nurse from the intensive care ward was on the line, explaining in a kind but weary voice that Jack was still unconscious.

'We're doing everything we can for him,' she said. 'But he's lost a lot of blood, and on top of his injuries he's very dehydrated and malnourished. If you give me your phone number I'll call back if anything changes.'

I thanked her, passed on my number, and rang off.

Shit. Jack was in a terrible condition. I had no idea whether he'd even make it through the night. He was my best – possibly only – chance to get the police to believe me.

My thoughts went back to the CCTV images the detectives had shown me. Why would Jack and Luke go off with a woman they didn't know? Unless they did know her? But none of us ever really went anywhere, so how on earth could they? And the red-light district – a prostitute? Surely not. But then I felt like I didn't know anything about anyone anymore. It seems I knew even less about my family than I realised. Maybe they had met that woman before, when they'd jumped out of the window to meet Oliver. Bloody Oliver. I didn't think anyone else would have introduced her to them. Everything kept coming back to him. And why the fuck was he up on Compington Mount this evening? I hadn't told the detectives about him being there because I'd wanted to do my own investigating before they called him in. Because once he was theirs I wouldn't get my own answers, and I needed those very badly.

It was time to visit Oliver in person. I knew where he lived, as he'd also written his address in the card he'd sent to Mum and Dad all those years ago. I was hoping he hadn't moved anywhere since – and I was soon going to find out. I wasn't going to tell him I was on the way, didn't want to give him any warning. He was proving to be as slippery as an eel. If he was involved in any of this and was intending on letting me take all the blame, he was about to be put straight. I still had the knife in my bag...

CHAPTER THIRTY

It was nearing eleven o'clock when I arrived outside the shabby red-brick apartment building that matched the address in the card. 68D St Anthony's Lane. My legs were hurting again, as I'd had to walk up a steep road to get there, one that rose high above the town centre. The residences had got seedier as I'd passed them, and I'd just seen three men fighting outside a pub. Clearly Oliver wasn't bothered about living in a good area, not like his dear sister. Our address was well thought of, apparently. Iris had, of course, mentioned this fairly frequently throughout our lives. I'd thought about visiting Hattie on the way, seeing as I still had her address in my pocket, but talking to Oliver was more urgent right now. Pushing away hints of apprehension and caution, I tried the main glass-panelled door. It was unlocked. I walked through, and stared at the letters on the doors. A, B and C. D must be up the careworn stairs.

Seconds later I'd nipped up to the first floor and was rapping on 68D's door. I could hear music playing inside and it stank of smoke and herbs where I stood on the landing. No answer. I knocked again, louder this time. Then I heard movement, and

Oliver opened the door. He did a double take when he saw me, then smiled. It looked forced. His eyes were wide and staring, his pupils massive, his hair ruffled and unkempt.

'Sophie, so glad you popped by,' he said. 'Come in.' He stepped backwards and waved his arm in an exaggerated welcoming gesture. I walked into his apartment without saying anything, hearing my uncle close the door behind me. It was a small place, and I immediately found myself in a messy, smoky living room. There were dirty plates and glasses on the floor, an overflowing ashtray on the arm of the threadbare sofa, chocolate wrappers and crisp packets on the cluttered coffee table. He was very different from Iris in so many ways. She'd have had a fit if she'd seen him living like this. We were never allowed to make a mess of any kind at home.

'Sit down, make yourself at home,' Oliver said, his voice weirdly loud. 'Do you want anything to drink? Tea? Coffee? Vodka?'

'No thanks,' I said, shoving a mess of clothes out of the way. 'I've come here to talk to you, Oliver. I need some answers.'

'Sure, sure,' he said, perching on the arm of the chair opposite. 'Fire away.' He reached towards the ashtray and picked up a strong-smelling rolled-up cigarette. 'Do you mind if I smoke my joint while you're here?'

I shook my head, watching him. Coughed, as the thick, herbal, woody smoke wafted over me. What a strange creature my uncle is, I thought. A middle-aged man with longish straggly hair, acting like a rebellious teenager all by himself in his flat. Maybe he's the type of person who never truly grows up. He must have bought the place with the inheritance that was shared between his sister and him; I couldn't imagine him holding down a proper, steady job for very long. I stared at the orange-and-brown-beaded bracelet on his wrist – it was something someone half his age would usually wear. I presumed he was alone, I couldn't see signs of anyone else being around. Which was good, as I needed to ask him some hard questions.

'What were you doing up on Compington Mount this evening?' I blurted out.

Oliver took a long drag, then filled the air with a stream of smoke.

'I could ask you the same question,' he said, letting his gaze rest on me. 'But fair enough, I'll go first. Basically, I was looking for something important.'

'What?' I said.

'Well, to be honest, you'd got me all alarmed before when you phoned, banging on about the police being interested in me,' he said, before taking another drag. I waited while he blew a few smoke rings. Coughed when they floated over to me. 'And the problem is, Sophie, that I gave your brothers something on Sunday evening that the police might well be interested in. They might find themselves compelled to trace it back to its original owner. And seeing as you said my Zippo lighter was found up on Compington Mount, I thought I'd better go and take a look for myself, and see if I could recover my goods.'

'Wait. What?' I said, letting his words sink in. 'You actually *saw my brothers* on Sunday evening?'

'Yep,' Oliver said with a grin. 'And they weren't very happy chappies, I can tell you. In a right state they were, all riled up and angry. They wanted me to give them something to help them calm down. So I did.'

'What did you give them?'

'Oh, just some medicinal marijuana that I had on me. And maybe a few other things.' Oliver inspected his joint. 'Great for soothing the nerves. You should try it sometime, Sophie.'

'No thanks,' I said, my tone coming out sharp. 'I take it you didn't tell the police you'd seen them?'

'Ah, no,' my uncle said, shaking his head. 'Like I explained to you on the phone, me and the police don't have the best relationship. And as I have no idea who attacked your brothers, it doesn't make a difference if I tell them or not, because I'm not the person they need to be looking for.'

I narrowed my eyes at him, but let this pass. For now. I needed him to keep talking.

'So what else did you give them, Oliver? Tell me, I need to know,' I said.

My uncle sighed and shifted his position.

'Look, you wouldn't understand,' he said. 'My sister kept you all so mollycoddled you have no idea about real life and its stresses and strains. Things can get hard sometimes you know, Sophie, and I've found that it just helps to have a few chemicals about to take the edge off the most taxing days.'

'What do you mean?' I said.

There was a pause.

'I gave your brothers something a bit stronger than pot too, to take away with them,' Oliver said, looking away.

'What?' I said, tempted to go over and shake him. His stupid remark about me being mollycoddled had stung; I'd wanted to tell him the truth at that point, shout in his face about the evil human being his sister had really been. But instead, I'd swallowed it down. I needed to find out what was going on, right now that was even more important. 'For fuck's sake, just tell me.' I knew that there were drugs in the world, Iris had shoved enough news articles in front of my face full of tragic stories about young drug users dying. I was aware of their evils. I mean, my own biological mother was a drug addict for God's sake. I was born addicted to crack cocaine.

'Heroin,' Oliver said, eventually. 'I gave them some brown, all right? But in my defence,' he said quickly, seeing the wrath come into my eyes, 'they asked me for something stronger than marijuana. Practically begged for it. Said they'd had a shit day –

were complaining about your parents – and needed to escape for a while. Mentally. Needed to put a buffer between them and the world. Heroin's the best thing for that.'

I closed my eyes, my head reeling, trying to slot all this new information into place.

'So you're telling me,' I said slowly, 'that you actually met up with Jack and Luke on Sunday evening, presumably after they'd jumped out of my dad's car?'

'Yep,' Oliver said.

'And you gave them a lot of drugs; marijuana and heroin? And your lighter?'

'Yeah. And I gave it to them in my special tin,' Oliver said. 'It just seemed easier at the time. The tin's distinctive, everyone on the scene knows it's mine. That's what I was looking for, it's what I keep my stuff in. I wanted to find it before the police did, because if they did get it, they'd be able to trace it and its contents straight back to me.'

I thought hard.

'And did you find it?' I said, opening my eyes. 'Your tin?'

'No.' Oliver shook his head. Worry flitted across his face.

'How the bloody hell did you meet up with my brothers on Sunday night?' I said. What he'd said still didn't make any sense to me. 'Luke got out of the car randomly, when Dad got stuck behind a truck. I was there, I saw what happened. They couldn't have planned it, it all unfolded spontaneously. And I know Luke had Dad's phone, so what did he do? Ring you at that point to come and meet them somewhere?'

I felt sad. I'd known my brothers jumped out of their window to smoke with Oliver sometimes, but I had no idea they were actually proper drug users. How uncaring of my uncle to introduce such harmful stuff into the twins' lives. What a family of broken dysfunctional people we were.

'No, it was a bit of a coincidence actually,' Oliver said,

leaning over to grab a lighter from the table. 'I was out with my girlfriend, and I spotted both the boys near the harbour.'

'Yeah, that's where Dad stopped,' I said.

'I was very surprised, as you lot are never out by yourselves. I waved at them and told Crystal I'd seen them,' Oliver said. 'She's been wanting to meet my family for ages, so I called them over but they didn't hear, they were talking to each other. So Crystal went over and got their attention. Had a word. When they came back with her, I realised how stressed they were, so we went somewhere quiet for a smoke and a chat. You know how it is.'

'And you just thought you'd leave me out on the road at night by myself, did you?' I said, my voice rising. 'Thanks very much, Uncle. So kind and caring of you.'

Oliver looked up, a startled expression on his face.

'I didn't know you were there, too, at that stage, Sophie,' he said. 'I promise, that's the truth. If I had, I'd have suggested you come with us as well. The boys didn't mention you or Rachel when I first met up with them, and from where I was standing I couldn't see you or the car. Luke and Jack were just so caught up with their own thoughts at that point – they didn't remember about you until after they'd had a smoke, then Jack jumped up – he became quite agitated at that point – and said we had to find you. He was insistent. So we walked back to the harbour but we couldn't see you anywhere. We looked around for ages, up and down roads, along the seafront, in late-night cafés and the nightclub. Even in the casino. Honestly.'

I considered his words while I studied his face. Oliver was a weak person, I decided. But he was telling the truth about this.

'Your girlfriend Crystal must be the woman I saw when the police showed me the CCTV then,' I said. 'What's her hair like?'

'Long and wavy,' Oliver said, his eyes snapping back onto

me. 'She's a beautiful, busty blonde. Just my type. What do you mean when the police showed you the CCTV?' His forehead was creasing up.

I almost laughed.

'Don't worry, Oliver, you and your drugs aren't on it,' I said. 'Only Crystal's back view is. Why were you and Crystal in that part of town anyway?'

'Crystal works there,' Oliver said, lighting his joint up again.

'What, in the red-light district?'

'Yep.' He nodded. 'But I know what you're thinking, and no, she's not a hooker. She works in a casino down there. That's where we met.'

I thought for a minute, about everything he'd told me, his secrecy, the drugs. The places he hung out, and the people he liked to mix with. His aversion to the police...

'Oliver, do you deal drugs as well as take them?'

He looked at me, then looked away, not saying anything.

'I'll take that as a yes,' I said with a sigh. I shook my head. 'So that's why you're so desperate to avoid the police. You're still a criminal, not just the teenage tearaway you made yourself out to be. Nice, Oliver. Very classy. Such a good role model.'

'Well, we all have our secrets,' Oliver said, turning towards me. 'We all have our shadow sides. Don't we, Sophie? Like, why were you up on Compington Mount earlier? And more to the point, how did you end up back in the car with Iris, Don and Rachel? It makes your version of what happened a bit more complicated, doesn't it?' My uncle narrowed his eyes at me.

I stood up.

'Like you were just saying, we all have our secrets,' I said, walking through his mess towards the door. 'And those are two of mine that I'm going to keep for a bit longer. Just one more thing, Oliver?' I turned, my hand on the door handle. 'What happened to my brothers after you gave them the drugs? Did you stay with them, or do you know where they went?'

'No, I didn't stay with them,' Oliver said. He'd followed me to the door and was standing very close to me now. 'I went back to my flat. Crystal went back to her job at the casino. The boys didn't tell me where they were going. They just left. I didn't think to ask. Look, I had no idea all this was going to happen, did I?'

He seemed so pathetic, with his big pupils and loud voice. I suddenly – for once – felt like the more dominant one in the room. The more intelligent, together person.

I leaned even closer to him, so that my face was a couple of inches away from his.

'If you're lying...' I said. 'If you know why Luke's dead and Jack's in a coma... I'll find out. And then I'll come back and see you. But I won't be such a good guest the next time. I need answers, and no one is being helpful. And if I find out that you're trying to frame me for something I didn't do, I'm going to sort that out and repair it *my* way. Okay?'

'Christ, you're as weird as your mother,' Oliver muttered as he ushered me out of his door. 'Iris was a bitch of a big sister when we were growing up. She pretty much tortured me when I was a child. And she used to threaten me all the time, like you just did.'

'You have no idea,' I said sweetly. He shook his head and closed the door. No one had any idea about me, I thought, jumping down the stairs, and I liked it that way. I was only just finding out who I really was myself. Coming to terms with the fact I was no longer a subdued, controlled child; that I now had more influence and power in me than I ever realised. There was still more I remembered about Sunday evening and Monday morning that I hadn't told a living soul. I was only just starting to admit it to myself. The memories were only just filtering back slowly, in fragments and bits. But I didn't have anything to do with anyone's deaths. Not really. And what mattered now was clearing my name so I could go on with the rest of my life freely. I may have made some strange decisions on Sunday evening, ones I didn't particularly care to think about, but I wasn't a murderer. No way. That much I knew. And after all, didn't Oliver say that everyone has a shadow side? I was only just coming to terms with mine...

CHAPTER THIRTY-ONE

I slept in late on Monday morning, and woke up to the sound of the doorbell incessantly ringing. Rubbing my eyes, I wandered downstairs and opened the door. Lisa was standing there. She was wearing her police uniform – she almost looked like a different person. Much more official and stern. My heart jumped and stress flooded my brain, waking me up in an instant.

'I was beginning to think you weren't in,' she said, stepping round me and walking into the house. 'I've come to ask you some questions, Sophie. Is that okay?'

'Sure,' I said. Didn't look like I had much of a choice.

Seconds later, we were seated at the kitchen table. I was now on high alert, my thoughts jostling to get into order. It was so important that I didn't make any mistakes with what I said now.

Lisa's radio crackled and she listened for a minute, her head cocked to one side. Then she looked back at the open notebook in front of her.

'Detective Warner and Detective Pierce have filled me in on the interview they conducted with you yesterday,' Lisa said, her tone all businesslike. 'I know what you told them, and I'm aware that they showed you the CCTV footage of you and your brothers exiting the SUV. They've asked me to do some follow-up questions with you, so I'll get started right away. We need to build the biggest possible picture of who you and your brother and sister and parents were and are, in order to understand the dynamics involved here. So to begin with, describe your parents' life – or what you know of it – before they adopted you. Who really were Iris and Don Macreavy?'

I sighed. This was not my favourite topic. But I opened my mouth and started talking, telling Lisa everything I knew about my parents' former lives, how lauded they were by the local church and community, how women were drawn to my mum and men to my dad; that they were everyone's golden couple. Well, most people's. I even got photos down from the living-room walls and showed Lisa the images of Iris and Don handing cheques to fundraising charities, with everyone around them clapping. How something had happened when I was younger that made them leave the church and set up their own one at home. I told her yet again, how she and the detectives needed to look into the people involved with that, and how I'd found out a bit about who was implicated in the rift. I got up, found some paper, copied out the list of names and contact details from my own list that I always kept in my pocket. I slid it across the table to her, and she folded it, putting it into her bag without looking at it.

'A very successful couple on the whole,' Lisa said, writing something in her notebook. I couldn't believe it. She'd completely ignored what I'd said about the church, and the problems there. But now didn't feel the right time to challenge her. She wouldn't listen to me anyway... 'And do you know if they ever had a biological child of their own, before you came along? Or did they try? Or perhaps they couldn't have children of their own. I'm only asking as it's important we know of all living relatives. We need to get in contact with anyone – everyone – in their lives.'

I blinked, thrown by her question.

'Er, no, not as far as I know,' I said slowly. 'I mean, Mum and Dad weren't very approachable, I learned very early on not to ask them personal questions, they didn't like it. They told me they couldn't have kids of their own, that's all. And I do know that Iris was desperate for children of her own, and really wanted to adopt. She told us that many times, before reminding us how lucky we were to have her and Don as parents.'

Lisa nodded, writing, her face impassive.

'And when you first came to live with them, what was life like for you?' she said, looking up.

I told her about Iris's natural strictness, but how my parents didn't punish or whip me in the way that they did when the other three arrived.

'You must have resented your new siblings for that,' Lisa said, staring into my eyes. 'Perhaps a part of you hated Jack, Luke and Rachel for messing up the life you had before they came on the scene? Wished they'd never arrived and that you still had your parents to yourself?'

I shifted, feeling uncomfortable. Because she wasn't exactly wrong, I had always borne a bit of a grudge against the other three – in my heart – because quite frankly my life had been a lot easier before they turned up. And that was the honest truth. I'd never been showered with love by Iris and Don, that just wasn't their style. But at least they still took me out and about with them then, and I went to school and had friends. Even going to church was better than being stuck at home. I'd had more freedom then. And I fully believed what Iris told me about how lucky I was to be with her and Don at that stage. That I would be a drug-addict child in the gutter if it wasn't for them.

And I'd have been happy to put up with the lack of love, if it meant I could lead a relatively normal life around that. I'd respected my parents at that point. But that version of my life stopped, because Iris couldn't cope when there were four of us. But I'd never wanted them dead. No way. I just wasn't that sort of person.

'Um...' I said. 'I mean, obviously life changed for me when they arrived. But the way Iris started behaving wasn't their fault, they didn't do anything wrong. It wasn't Rachel or Luke or Jack's fault that she became so controlling and violent. Don was okay at first – he used to smuggle snacks up to us when Iris withheld food. But she got annoyed with his kinder attitude so he slowly changed. Became more like her.'

Lisa narrowed her eyes at me, but didn't say anything. She just looked down and scribbled away in her notebook.

'And do you have any contact with your birth family at the moment?' she said, glancing up again. 'Your biological mother or father, for example? Or any extended relatives?'

'No,' I said. 'I haven't seen any of them since I was adopted. I have no idea where they are now. Iris made it very clear that I wasn't to ask questions about them.'

'Okay. I will be checking into that,' Lisa muttered. Passive-aggressive, I decided. That's what Dad would have labelled her. But she wasn't when she'd first come to see me at the hospital. She'd been so lovely and kind then...

As I watched her write, an uncontrollable anger seethed up in me again. Hide it, I told myself. Don't let her see how you feel, Sophie. But the unfairness of how she was treating me now had suddenly become overwhelming. The bile was too strong, too powerful this time. I swallowed and coughed, trying to shake it away. Lisa and the other detectives clearly thought I'd somehow ended the lives of most of my family. The woman in front of me had morphed from being a kind and warm supportive friend, to being my biggest foe, my accuser, who now looked at me with suspicion. And the horrible thing was, the change in Lisa was my fault, I knew it was. If only I'd been able to be straightforward with her and the detectives from the start, none of this would have happened. But I'd felt so confused at the time, so locked in to myself. I hadn't been able to make my mind process the events of Sunday night, so I'd chosen to go into denial and say I remembered nothing. I thought it would be easier. It turns out it wasn't.

'Right.' Lisa finished her notes and looked up at me. 'I believe your grandparents on both your adoptive mother and father's sides have passed away?'

I nodded. I'd never met any of them.

'And that your uncle, Oliver, is your only known relative that you're aware of?'

I nodded again. Dad had been an only child, and Mum just had one brother.

'And when was the last time you saw him – your uncle?'

I already had an answer worked out for this question; at least I'd had enough time to prepare for this shot, work out my reaction. I felt in my bones that there was still more that my druggie uncle wasn't telling me, and I wanted to do my own digging before I implicated him. Because if I gave Lisa any ammunition about Oliver, I knew she would tie me into it somehow, as she'd already said she thought we were both involved. So there was no way I was planning to do that. I knew I was a lone wolf now, I had to look after myself. I'd accepted that. I was totally on my own. The police weren't going to help me, in fact they wanted to blame me. So I was going to put the pieces of the puzzle together my way. And if that meant hiding information from Lisa, then so be it.

'Oh.' I wrinkled my forehead, trying to look as though I was searching my memory. 'Quite a while ago. It must have been at least two months since I saw Oliver. Yes, that's it. I remember him coming over when it was still very hot in the summertime.'

Lisa stared at me without talking. Then slowly nodded her head.

'Sure,' she said. 'If you say so.'

That was weird. What did she mean, if I say so? There was no way she could have known I saw Oliver the night before; I'd been really careful, made sure I wasn't being followed, had looked around me the whole time I was walking. And I knew Oliver wouldn't have told her, as he seemed practically allergic to the police. And he'd said she'd never contacted him, that the only two police officers that had come to see him about the murders were male. Although he could be lying, of course...

Lisa asked me a few more questions before she left, about what my real feelings were towards my siblings and my parents, about how my parents had truly treated us – she seemed to be questioning my claims that they were abusive, which felt insulting – and about if I'd ever fantasised about having the whole lot of them out of the picture so I could get on with life my way. I kept my answers brief; I loved my siblings, my parents really were abusive in many, many ways, and no, I definitely didn't want my whole family to die. Not even Iris and Don. They may have acted like monsters, and I may be a bit messed up in the head, but I was no murderer. I wasn't sorry I hadn't clearly told the truth from the start, but I was now. (Mostly, I added silently. Actually, if truth be told, I was omitting something quite significant that I remembered, but I would never tell anyone about that bit. Ever.)

Then Lisa closed her notebook and stood up, making her chair scratch on the kitchen tiles.

'Thanks for answering my questions, Sophie,' she said, her radio crackling again. 'Obviously, as I'm sure you know, it doesn't look good for you or Oliver, does it?'

'What do you mean?' I said, also standing up.

Lisa's eyes were hard.

'You know what I mean,' she said. 'You and I both know that you and Oliver were responsible for what happened to all your family members. We still don't know which one of you murdered Don, Iris and Rachel, but we'll find out. You or Oliver killed Luke, and you both tried your hardest to do away with Jack. So don't get too comfortable with your new free life, Sophie, because I can assure you it won't be lasting for much longer.'

The anger – that I'd been keeping under wraps – burst up and out; the toxic lava flow was finally free.

'For fuck's sake, Lisa,' I shouted. 'I didn't do any of this. You have the wrong person. Stop saying it was me; it wasn't. The other detectives said they aren't treating me as their main suspect, and they said they have no evidence against me.'

'And you believed them?' Lisa said, a smirk playing on her lips. 'Think about it, Sophie. Good cop, bad cop isn't just a movie thing. Police do it in real life too. It helps to squeeze information out of suspects. Like I said. We know it was you, and don't think about running off because I'll find you, wherever you go.'

And with that, she turned and walked out of my house.

CHAPTER THIRTY-TWO

I was so incensed, so crazy and angry, that I walked out too. I slammed the door shut, then stormed past Mr Finney, peeping through his net curtains next to a large statue of what looked like the Virgin Mary – funny, I'd never noticed he had that there before – past Lisa's car; I was tempted to kick it but managed not to, and kept walking. My thoughts were hot, fuzzy; it felt as though a fire of wrath was raging in my brain. How dare she accuse me like that? How *dare* she?

On and on I went. I lost track of time, I had no idea where I was going. I just knew I needed to keep walking until the white-hot rage in me had subsided, because if I went back to the house too soon, God knows what I would do. I wanted to trash things, destroy them. Purge my anger by transferring it into destruction.

Raindrops started to fall, soaking my hair, but I didn't care. They calmed me down, their wet coldness helped to extinguish the biggest part of the fiery rage in me. And eventually, I got my phone out and saw that I'd been walking for over two hours. I used Google Maps to get me back home.

That's when I saw what had happened. Someone had been in my house while I'd been out.

CHAPTER THIRTY-THREE

The front door was open. I stopped and stared at it. I knew I'd shut it, because I remember slamming it as hard as I could when I left, and hearing the latch click into place. As far as I knew, no one else had a key. We were never allowed them when Iris and Don were alive; mainly because we were kept as prisoners and forbidden from going anywhere. Jack was still unconscious in hospital. The police might have a key, but I'd seen Lisa's car drive past me while I was stomping along; and anyway, why would she have reason to go back into my house while I wasn't there?

I thought about calling the police, and asking them to come and check the house – see if anyone was still inside. But there didn't seem to be any point. They already had me pinned as a potential murderer; I was quite sure that they would use any further information against me. Perhaps they would accuse me of making up the break-in, or of wasting police time.

So instead, I took two steps into the house, leaving the front door open behind me. I stood very still, listening. If anyone was still inside, I was hoping they'd make a noise; give themselves away. But I heard nothing. Only the sounds of cars driving down the road behind me.

Very slowly, I examined each room in the house. There was no one downstairs; I made sure I opened all the cupboards, even ones far too small or crowded to fit a person inside. Then I tiptoed upstairs, and looked in the boys' room and my parents' bedroom. Still no sign of anyone.

I pushed the door of my own bedroom open, and stopped.

Someone had been in there. My new duvet – I'd appropriated the one from my parents' bed since coming home – was messed up and thrown to one side. When I'd left my bed to open the door for Lisa, I hadn't left it like that; the duvet had still been laid out on my mat. But someone had thrown my mat around too; it was now curled up haphazardly under the window. My sparse belongings were strewn across the mess on the floor, just chucked around. What the actual fuck?

Then I saw it out of the corner of my eye. I bent down, and picked it up. An orange-and-brown beaded bracelet. I'd seen it just the night before; I knew exactly who it belonged to.

CHAPTER THIRTY-FOUR

Oliver must have broken into my house, I thought, jogging down the stairs. There was no other explanation. Or had Don and Iris given him a key for safekeeping in the past, in case they lost theirs? People did that kind of thing, didn't they? And he was in my room, maybe looking for something. But what? Me? My phone? Money? His stupid drug box? His bracelet must have fallen off without him realising, before he'd left. I grabbed my rucksack, a drink and food, and my phone and keys, and left the house, taking care to slam the door behind me. I checked it was locked three times.

Then I set off in the direction of Oliver's flat. The fury was back, and this time it was channelled directly at my uncle. He'd already proved to be an untrustworthy drug dealer who only looked after his own interests. And now I find that he's been in my house? And yes, it was my house now; that's how I thought of it. Bloody hell, I'd earnt that privilege, hadn't I? Putting up with Iris and Don's treatment for so many years. It was the least they could do – leave me a place to live now that they were dead.

Half an hour later, I was running up the stairs to Oliver's

flat, panting. But I wasn't tired this time, I had too much adrenaline coursing through my veins for that. I banged on the door of 68D, then kicked it for good measure.

'All right, all right.' Oliver's voice was slurry and slow. 'Stop kicking my bloody door, whoever you are.'

The door opened a crack, but the key chain was on. I could see one of Oliver's eyes peering at me.

'Open the door,' I said loudly. 'I'm coming in.'

'Jesus, keep your knickers on,' Oliver said. He closed the door to, and I heard the chain sliding out of place. He opened it more fully, and I barged in, immediately taking in the scene in front of me.

There were four slumbering bodies in his living room. Two on the sofa, one in the armchair and one on the floor. I looked round at my uncle, and saw that his hair was standing on end. He was rubbing his eyes. Either he'd just woken up, or he was really great at acting. The room stank of what I now knew was pot. Little silver foil wraps were scattered around on his messy coffee table, and I knew at once the five of them had been taking much harder drugs than marijuana. Losers.

I let out an infuriated groan. Nothing was making sense.

'Did you just break into my house?' I shouted at him, not caring that two of the sleepers raised their heads to see what was going on.

'What?' Oliver said, his eyes widening. He ran a hand through his long, greasy hair.

'Did you come round and go into my house, about an hour ago?' I said, stepping towards him. 'And don't lie. I found this in my bedroom.' I pulled his bracelet out of my jacket pocket and brandished it in the air. 'I know it's yours, I saw you wearing it yesterday evening, so don't lie.'

My uncle looked at the bracelet, and then back at me.

'Yes, that is mine,' he said. 'I wondered where it went. And no, I did not just break into your house, Sophie. I've been barely able to move for the last five hours. My friends came round after you left yesterday and we ended up having a heavier than expected night. Ask any of them. I haven't left my apartment since you left yourself.'

I stared at him, feeling crazy. Because every bit of evidence in front of me was pointing to his words being true. But that made everything more confusing. How the fuck did his bracelet end up in my room?

'Well, if you haven't left your flat since yesterday, how did this get into my house then?' I said, waving the bracelet. 'Hmm?'

Oliver looked as bewildered as I felt.

He sighed, splaying out his hands.

'Look, I really don't know,' he said. 'For all I know, Sophie, you might have gone mad and taken my bracelet last night without me knowing, and be trying to frame me for something. I have no idea how it ended up in your house, I really don't.'

'Don't be stupid, you were wearing your bracelet yesterday evening,' I said, spitting my words out. 'How on earth could I have taken it off your wrist without you realising? You weren't that fucked at the time. That's just ridiculous. So are you telling me, that the only people you've seen since yesterday, apart from me, are these four who are in your flat right now?'

Oliver nodded.

'Yes,' he said. 'Oh, and my girlfriend, Crystal. She popped in for a couple of hours at around one, had a bit of fun with us. Then she left, as she had to go to work.'

I raised my eyebrows.

'The casino she works in stays open all night,' Oliver said. 'Her work hours are always insane.'

'And you said you met her when she was working at the casino?' I said. 'How long have you known Crystal? Do you trust her?'

Oliver laughed.

'Yes, of course I trust her,' he said. 'She's a great girl, really feisty. I've known her for nearly six months now, and I can tell you that there's nothing dodgy about her, Sophie. Crystal works hard and plays hard; just the kind of girl I like.'

I sighed. Nothing was adding up. I was starting to feel like I'd fallen down a rabbit hole that led to a world where everyone was mad. Or maybe it was just me who was?

'I haven't been having the best day so far,' I said. 'That policewoman, Lisa Denton, came round again. She started firing questions at me about my life, and about Iris and Don. She was asking really stupid things, like did they ever have any biological children of their own. I said no, obviously. Otherwise why would they have adopted me and the other poor sods? And what relevance would that have to the case anyway?'

'Ah,' Oliver said. 'Did Iris not ever tell you?'

'Tell me what?' I looked at him. 'Iris never shared anything with me, Oliver. You have no idea what she put me and the other three through. We were never allowed to know a single thing about her and Don's past.'

'That doesn't surprise me,' he said, shaking his head. 'She's always been like that. She was a strange creature when we were younger. So closed in and secretive. She barely told me anything either, even when we were both adults. But there is something I know, that was too big – literally – even for her to hide.'

'What?' I said.

'Iris did have a baby, long before you four came into her life,' Oliver said, leaning against the wall. 'It wasn't planned, and Don wasn't the father. She was with this musician guy for a few months, their relationship was stormy and he left her. But then she found out she was expecting his child. She had no money at that time, and didn't want the baby, so she decided to give it up to social care. She never told me any of this, of course. I wouldn't have found out unless I'd gone to visit her unexpectedly when she was nine months pregnant. I needed to ask her for some favour or other. I couldn't believe my eyes when I saw the size of her belly.'

'And she told you she was going to give the baby up to social services?' I said, feeling my eyes getting wider as I spoke. Wow. This was some news I never expected.

'Yep,' Oliver said. 'She explained that she just wasn't in a good position to look after it. And she was right, she wasn't. She had no money, and no one to support her. Our parents weren't much use. They were alive at that time, but they were so traditional and Catholic; if she'd told them she'd had a baby out of wedlock they'd have disowned her, and she knew it.'

'And was the baby a girl or a boy?' I said. I wanted to find out as much as I could about Iris's secret former life, this secret she'd hidden among many.

'A boy, I think,' Oliver said. 'I never met him, the baby was removed from her care while she was still in the hospital and as far as I know she never saw him again. I tried to ask her about the whole thing years later to make sure she was okay about what had happened, but she wouldn't talk about it. I'm not even sure if Don knew.'

'Oh my God,' I said, as the news sank in. 'I can't believe she never told us about that. She always said her and Don couldn't have kids of their own. Actually, I can believe she hid it. Like I said, she never shared anything with us.' My mind was now whirring, assessing all possibilities... Was the baby Jason – Lisa's boyfriend? Was it a member of the church that Iris and Don had left? Someone I didn't know at all? A person who now held a grudge against her and was out to get us all? Did Oliver know more than he was letting on?

'That sounds like Iris,' Oliver said, rolling his eyes.

We paused for a minute, both lost in thought.

'Okay,' I said eventually, shifting position, trying to get my brain together. 'Fine. So I believe you were here all night and all day. By the way, you should really have a shower soon, Oliver, you look like a state. And it stinks in here.'

'Thank you,' he said with a grin.

The adrenaline was leaving my body as fast as it had come in. I was feeling defeated, deflated. I'd been so sure I was going to catch my uncle out, and get some concrete evidence showing that he was involved in my family's deaths that I could take to the police. But instead, I now had more questions than answers. My bones felt heavy now. I wanted to go home. Fall into a deep sleep.

I said my goodbyes, and set off back to Bridge Avenue through the late afternoon October cold and drizzle.

As I reached the bottom of his long sloping road, and rounded the corner by the pub, I suddenly came to a halt. A thought that needed more attention had entered my mind.

If Oliver hadn't broken into my house, then who had? The most logical person to suspect – the person who'd been in the kitchen with me earlier today, and who'd had a chance to make a copy of my front door key before handing it over to me – was Lisa. She'd known I'd left the house, she'd driven past me as I walked down the road. She knew the place was empty. But why the actual hell would she go into my house and mess up my bedroom? And there was absolutely no way she could have got hold of Oliver's bracelet. It didn't make sense. It was just impossible. Wasn't it?

CHAPTER THIRTY-FIVE

Back at home, I made a cup of tea and ate some toast. I was still skinny, I thought, looking down at my drainpipe legs, but my face had lost its skeletal look since I'd been living in the house by myself. Food didn't really interest me, I'd had to force myself not to think about hunger for so long that I'd lost any delight in it. But I had been eating a bit more than when Iris and Don were alive, and from what I saw in the mirror when I went to the bathroom, I was looking better for it. Less wizened, stronger – my cheeks – amid the healing scars – were rosier.

I got my phone out and sat down at the table. I went on to Facebook, and found Lisa Denton's page – Lisa Jane. As before, I could hardly access any information at all on it, just the photo of her and her partner Jason Stewart. I couldn't even see her friend list. I clicked on Jason's page again, determined to do a forensic examination of it. I needed to know everything I could about this woman who was accusing me of murder.

This time, I scrolled back through more of his photos. He didn't seem to have many privacy settings on his account, all his information was there for the world to see, which I was glad about. There were more snaps of him and Lisa together in uniform, or out with mates. Ah, there was one with Lisa looking a bit different. Her hair was lighter and longer and she looked a bit younger. They must have been together for a while then. I kept going. Ah, now that was interesting. An image of Lisa with very blonde hair popped up. It suited her, even more than the brown did. She really was very pretty, in a sharp, angular kind of way, I reflected. I kept trawling through Jason's photos, until they stopped showing Lisa and started showing him at police training college. None of her there, he must have met her after he'd graduated.

I turned my attention to Jason's friend list. Bloody hell, the man knew eight hundred and sixty-four people. It put my own Melody Brown page to shame – I was up to thirty-eight friends. Zach still hadn't read my messages, and now I could put the hurt that he caused me into a little box far away in my soul, where it would never be looked at or touched. He'd let me down, but I'd accepted that it was just me against the world now. I didn't need him or anyone else. Bastard.

I read down the endless list of his friends' names. Some of them sounded weird – like Jelly Starfish and Hammertime. A few seconds later, I stopped, and did a double take at the name that had appeared in front of me. I couldn't believe it. But yes, it really did say what I thought it said. Jason, Lisa Denton's boyfriend, was friends with Iris Macreavy on Facebook. He was connected to my dead mother. A thrill of fear shook through my body. Could Iris's biological baby really be him? Had he tracked her down – angry that she'd given him up? Could he be the one punishing my family?

CHAPTER THIRTY-SIX

B ut, I quickly rationalised – immediately squashing the terror down – it wasn't that surprising really, was it, that he knew of my mother? Iris was Facebook friends with practically everyone in Torquay; she was one half of the community's golden couple after all. And her Facebook page and social standing were legendary. And when that photo of me and Brianna Salotto – taken at the Destruction Revolution rally – had gone viral, Iris had become almost famous. I'd read through the posts on her Facebook page from that time after I'd joined as Melody Brown, and they'd made me sick to my stomach. She'd posted that snap of Brianna and me on her page – obviously – and it had over 47,000 likes. People had written things like, 'Wow, such a special child. You must be a wonderful mother'. And Iris had answered their posts in full narcissistic flow: 'I'm so proud of Sophie, our little drug baby. She's come so far since being born with crack flowing through her little veins. Just look at her now, growing into her own person and making a difference in the world. Where would she be now without us? I dread to think'.

Reading Iris's posts had made me understand something.

She didn't adopt my siblings and I because she wanted to love us and nurture us as her own children; she collected and used us to bolster her own public image as a caring, benevolent, superwoman. It had never been about us, it had always been about her. I reckoned that her biological son, whoever he was – Jason? – had got off lightly. My head was still spinning about that bit of information. He'd most probably been adopted by a wonderful couple and been given a great life. Good for him. Bad for us.

So when you considered all that, it wasn't really very surprising or meaningful that Jason was friends with my mother on social media. I quickly flicked over to her Facebook page. Yep, just as I thought, Iris Macreavy had 52,308 friends. Definitely most of Torquay. I felt relieved as the moment of panic in me subsided. But I filed the information away, I couldn't altogether discount it. But it didn't need to make me panic as much as it initially had. I had to remember that Jason and Lisa were both respected police officers, and that Lisa was just doing her job. It was mostly my fault that she'd changed her opinion of me so drastically and quickly – I'd never been very good at telling the truth, and now I was facing the consequences. She was wrong about me, she was accusing me of something terrible that I didn't do. But maybe she had every right to be suspicious of me; I'd confused the police with my changing stories about what I could remember from Monday night. I wasn't even telling the whole truth now. I couldn't even face it myself. Denial was the easiest option. But I knew I was definitely not a murderer.

My phone bleeped into life, making me jump. I answered it.

'Hello,' said a man's voice. 'Can I speak to Sophie Macreavy, please?'

'Yes, it's me,' I said.

'Oh hello, Sophie, this is Ali Kaur, I'm the charge nurse on the ITU. I'm just phoning with some good news. Your brother Jack opened his eyes about an hour ago. He still can't speak at the moment, but he's awake, and his condition is slowly improving. If you'd like to come and visit him, I can let you into the ward for an hour, but no longer at the moment, I'm afraid.'

I felt a smile wash across my lips.

'That's fantastic news,' I said. 'Thank you so much for letting me know. Yes, I'll come and visit Jack. Is it okay if I come now? It will take me about forty-five minutes to get there.'

'Yes that's fine,' Ali said. 'When you get to the hospital just ask for directions to the ICU at reception.'

I said goodbye and rang off, feeling elated. Suddenly I wasn't tired anymore; the adrenaline was back and pumping round my body with full force. Jack was awake. He was getting better. Soon, he might be able to talk. And then he could tell the police I had nothing to do with the murders – he would explain who had attacked him and Luke. And everything would be okay. This was fabulous news. I grabbed my rucksack and headed for the door.

CHAPTER THIRTY-SEVEN

It was just before six when I arrived at the hospital. The rain had stopped about ten minutes before I'd arrived, and my hair was wet, plastered down either side of my face. The man at the reception desk gave me directions to the ICU while staring at my facial scars and a few minutes later I arrived outside its doors. I pressed the buzzer, and waited.

A nurse let me in, and took me to Jack's cubicle. The now familiar antiseptic scent was strong in here. I felt the same as I had up on Compington Mount: the boy in the bed looked nothing like my brother. His face was so swollen that his right eye was just a slit, his nose looked mangled, and there were bruises and wounds on every bit of flesh that I could see. Tubes ran from his cannula to the bar above his bed, attached to bags of blood and fluids. Monitors beeped next to him, their lights flashing rhythmically. The eye I could see clearly was shut.

'Jack can't talk at the moment,' the nurse told me, although I already knew this. 'But if you go over and hold his hand, I'm sure he'll be glad to see you. The sense of touch is very important to our patients; it really helps with their recovery.'

I did what she said. I walked over and rested my hand

lightly on top of Jack's, avoiding the wound on his wrist. His left eye flickered and opened. He looked at me, and the beeping on the monitor next to him sped up.

'Hey, it's okay,' I said softly. 'It's me, Sophie. I've come to see you. I'm so glad you're alive, Jack.'

My brother moved his head from one side to the other. It seemed to be the only part of his body he could move easily. Why was he doing that? Was he trying to tell me something?

'What is it, Jack?' I was trying to keep my voice calm. I could see the ends of other patient's beds sticking out of cubicles. This place had such a calm, sterile atmosphere; I felt very aware of the need for quietness. I didn't want to upset my brother, but at the same time, he seemed to want to communicate something.

Jack made a noise. His mouth didn't open, but a low noise came out. His left eye stared at me. What was he trying to get me to understand?

'Do you want to tell me something?' I said.

His head gave a faint nod.

'Okay,' I said. 'Is it something about who did this to you?'

Another barely visible nod.

'Was it Uncle Oliver?'

Jack stayed still for a minute; maybe he was surprised by my question. Then a small shake of the head.

I exhaled. Wow. At least I had one answer amid the chaos of it all now.

I felt movement behind me, and turned to find a woman wearing scrubs approaching.

'Hi, I'm Doctor Musa,' she said. 'You must be Jack's sister? The nurse told me you were coming.'

I nodded.

'Jack's in a very serious condition,' Doctor Musa said. 'He's lucky to be alive. He sustained a multitude of injuries in the attack on him, and will have to undergo at least two operations when his condition has stabilised further. But the signs are so far good. I think we can be cautiously optimistic that he will make some sort of recovery, although at this stage I can't say what the lasting impact on him will be.'

I nodded again, trying to take in everything she was saying.

'I know you've only just arrived to see your brother,' Doctor Musa said. 'And I'm so sorry, but we're going to have to take him back downstairs for another CT scan. One of our consultants thinks she may have spotted another skull fracture on his first scan – we already know he has four, but it could be five – and it's important we get this done as soon as possible. I'm sure you can come back tomorrow for at least an hour, if you are able.'

I looked down at Jack. I wished the doctor hadn't come over and said this; my brother had been trying to convey to me the identity of his attacker. I'd been so close to finding out the truth. But there was nothing I could do.

I gave a small smile.

'Of course,' I said. I touched Jack's hand. 'I'll be back tomorrow, okay? You keep getting better.'

Jack's left eye blinked in response.

It was only when I'd left the ward, and was making my way back towards the reception area, that I saw her. Officer Lisa Denton, queuing up in the hospital café. She had her back to me, and I was pretty sure she didn't see me. But I saw *her* all right. I hovered for a minute or two, making sure it really was Lisa; looked at her from the side for a few seconds. Yep, it was definitely my former family liaison officer, fully decked out in her police uniform.

Why the fuck was she here?

CHAPTER THIRTY-EIGHT

Yes, of course – she's here to see Jack, I told myself. That's what police do in an investigation, they support the victims of crime, and interview them when they are well enough to talk. But something felt wrong about Lisa being there at that time in the evening. I couldn't immediately put my finger on what it was; was it that she seemed to be there alone? I couldn't see any other officers around. Was it that Jack couldn't talk yet – and I knew the hospital staff would have made that very clear to the police, as they had done to me? So even if she wanted to interview him, she wouldn't be able to.

A very strange feeling came over me, as I took one last glance at Lisa's back, before walking fast towards the doors. Something about this whole investigation was wrong. I didn't know exactly what it was; but something was most definitely not right. It was just a sense that had been creeping up on me for a few days now; a feeling – an awareness. I not only felt like I was being set up – framed – for a crime I didn't commit, I most definitely felt – knew – that there was corruption afoot around me. Although admittedly I did feel guilty and responsible for the fact I hadn't been immediately honest with the police about everything. But the detectives and Lisa believed that I was guilty, and that if things went on the way they were going, the situation would end extremely badly for me. Who was setting me up? That was the question at the core of it all. Oliver? Even Lisa? Someone else in the police, like Lisa's partner Jason? After all, he was friends with my darling mother. Someone who hated Iris and Don from their old church? I needed to find out what exactly happened to make them leave. Even Jack? Although I thought that was very unlikely. Someone from my birth family? Someone I didn't know? Were they all in cahoots together?

Okay, I thought, turning out of the hospital's brightly lit car park and onto the much darker pavement. I'm becoming paranoid now. I have to stop thinking crazy thoughts and get my head together. Remember, Sophie, it's just you against the world now. You can't rely on anyone else. You have to keep your wits together or you're fucked.

CHAPTER THIRTY-NINE

'Hi, Sophie?'

I rubbed my eyes, trying to wake up. It was Tuesday morning. My ringing phone had just ended my deep sleep.

'Er, yep?'

'It's Lisa. I just wanted to let you know that your uncle Oliver has been taken into custody. He's being investigated in connection with the deaths of Iris, Don and Rachel, and with the murder of Luke.'

'*What?*' I said, sitting up.

'New DNA evidence has come to light,' Lisa said. 'And police arrested him at his flat earlier this morning.'

'What DNA evidence?' I said, trying to take it all in.

'I'm afraid I can't say any more at this time,' Lisa said. I heard some rustling, as though she was walking somewhere.

'So now it's only a matter of time before you're arrested too,' she said in a much lower voice. 'I'll leave you to think about that, Sophie.'

She rung off.

Okay, this was too much, I thought, throwing my phone down on the duvet. Yesterday when I'd seen Jack, I'd asked him if Oliver was responsible for hurting him, and he'd said no. So why had DNA evidence connected my uncle to these incidents? It just didn't make sense. And she was still threatening me; this woman who I'd seen at the hospital last night. This police officer, Lisa Denton.

Ten minutes later, I was down in the kitchen drinking coffee and eating toast. I now had no doubt that it was only a matter of time before I was arrested too, and this realisation had given rise to a fiery energy in my brain. I may have withheld the truth for too long, and I may still not be admitting to everything I knew – even to myself. It was too hard, it was impossible. But one thing I did know was that I wasn't responsible for the deaths. Yes, Lisa was telling me I was as good as guilty. Just as I'd told the detectives.

Time was running out. I needed to act fast, or I wouldn't have a chance to clear my name ever again. If I was arrested and found responsible my life would be over. I'd be back in a cell – this time a jail one – and I knew I wouldn't be able to cope with that. Abandoned and alone. I'd shrivel up and die; I knew I would.

I phoned the hospital and asked when I could visit my brother. They told me to be there in an hour, at eleven o'clock. The best thing was that they told me Jack had started talking, just a few words here and there. That he'd said he wanted to see me, been quite insistent about it apparently. I rung off and grabbed my bag, shoved the necessaries inside it. Jack was my last and only hope, and he could talk now. He could tell me about who was responsible for attacking him. I was so excited, my tummy was doing backflips. Finally, I'd know who the psycho behind all this was...

CHAPTER FORTY

As I walked between the cars in the hospital car park, I looked at my phone and saw it was five to eleven. Glancing up at the main front door – about one hundred yards away from where I was standing – I saw a familiar face. Lisa. She was walking quickly out and away from the hospital. This time in civilian clothes, not her uniform.

Instinctively, I ducked down so she didn't catch sight of me. But she wasn't looking around, she seemed to be lost in deep thought as she made her way to the right of the car park, away from me.

I stayed where I was until it was past eleven. I needed to remain undetected. But she must have gone by now? If I didn't hurry up I'd lose more valuable visiting time with my brother; and the nurse had told me I'd only get an hour as it was. Jack could talk, and he had some very important information I needed to hear...

Minutes later, I was standing outside the ITU, waiting to be buzzed in. This time it was a nurse who opened the door.

'Hi, I'm here to see Jack Macreavy?' I said, stepping through the door.

'Ah,' he said, a frown suddenly darkening his expression. 'Please, wait here for a minute. I'll find someone who can talk to you.'

What was going on?

Soon, the nurse that opened the door to me yesterday was walking towards me.

'Sophie?' she said. I nodded.

'I'm so sorry to tell you this,' she said. She was looking worried. 'But Jack's condition has just rapidly declined. We don't understand it ourselves. He was doing really well, he actually said a few words this morning after breakfast – he asked to see you. But over the last half an hour he slipped back into a coma. The doctors are examining him now, and making sure he is as comfortable as possible.'

A strong dizziness washed through me, and I stepped sideways, reaching out for the wall.

'Can I see him?' I said.

'No, I'm sorry,' the nurse said, shaking her head. 'He's not allowed visitors at the moment, his condition is too critical. The doctors are doing everything they can to stabilise him again. I know this must be so hard for you. I have your number – I'll phone you straightaway if there's any change.'

'Can I just ask something,' I said. 'By any chance, did anyone else come and see Jack today before I arrived?' I knew what her answer would be before she spoke.

'Yes,' the nurse said. 'The same policewoman as yesterday popped by. She said she had a couple of follow-up questions for him. Luckily she managed to talk to him before his condition deteriorated.'

I don't know how I made it back to the reception area again. A horrible understanding was now sitting centre stage in my brain. Lisa had done something bad to Jack. The lying, manipulative, murderous bitch.

CHAPTER FORTY-ONE

I pushed through the main hospital doors, my thoughts whirling. But why would Lisa do something to Jack? Surely it was no coincidence that he had started to talk this morning – the most obvious conclusion was that she wanted to silence him. But why? Surely Lisa couldn't be responsible for all the deaths in my family? What reason would a police officer who was totally unconnected to us, and who we'd never met before, have for doing this? Lisa didn't seem mad or psychotic to me; she was calm and rational. Therefore there must be a very compelling motive behind her actions. Perhaps she was covering for someone? Jason? It just didn't make sense.

The hospital car park was busy. I barely looked at anyone as I made my way through it towards the exit. But something at the edge of my vision caught my attention. I glanced over. Lisa was standing a few cars away, staring straight at me.

I broke into a run. Instinctively I knew I had to get far away from this woman. I didn't understand why she involved herself with my crazy fucked-up family, or what her level of participation was with all the deaths. I just knew for certain now that Lisa had bad – dangerous – intentions towards me. And she had just done something horrible to my brother. She'd harmed him. Had she wanted him dead? She must have.

I ran for what seemed like ages. Not in the direction of my house – that would be too obvious – she'd know exactly where to find me. I had no idea where I was going, but I purposefully turned down roads I didn't recognise at all, and cut through alleys that seemed secret and away from public view. I *was* in danger. A lot of it. Lisa was my enemy. And she knew absolutely everything about me. Why didn't I realise this before? Eventually a feeling of nausea overtook me and I had to stop. I was away from the main roads, at the top of a leafy path that dropped down sharply in front of me.

When I'd finished gulping air and my breathing had returned to something near normal – the nausea subsiding – I looked around me once again and set off down the unkempt path. The steep gradient made my feet hurt, as my toes were being pushed against the end of my trainers, but I didn't have time to worry about that now. I needed to get to a place of safety and solitude so I could figure out what the hell to do next. I needed to be far away from everyone, but most of all, away from Lisa.

I heard two male voices coming up the path the other way and I froze. Everyone seemed like a threat right now. Two middle-aged guys holding fishing rods came round the bend and walked past me, barely glancing in my direction. Shit, I was cracking up.

I continued on down the increasingly bumpy, gravelly trail; round overgrown bends with dense woodland either side. Suddenly I walked out of the undergrowth and saw the sea in front of me. I stopped, unaware I'd been so close to it, struck for a moment by its solemn beauty. The pale sunlight illuminated the calm waves in a hazy way. The grey water looked so calm and unruffled. Good. This was exactly where I needed to be in order to think.

Soon, with many glances around me, I'd made my way along the narrow coastal path and over some giant rocks. The whole side of the cliff seemed to be made up from them. Below me there was a pebbly beach, a dog and its owner making their way along the shoreline. I had no intention of doing anything as obvious as going down there, I wanted complete privacy, so I continued along the top of the rocks until I found a crevice I could sit in. I could still see the sea, but no one could spot me from where I was nestled. The air was salty and fresh and I took advantage of it, taking deep breaths. I needed all the clarity I could muster.

I stared at the horizon. Right. Things had gone from fucked up to even worse. Lisa had done something to Jack to make him slip back into a coma – I knew she had. Even if I had no way to prove it yet. Oliver was in custody, the bodies of Iris, Don, Rachel and Luke still lay in the morgue. And as Lisa had so blatantly pointed out: I would be the next one to be arrested. How had she done this? Why? My head was reeling. I felt beyond shocked and betrayed.

My phone bleeped into life in my pocket. I answered it.

'Hello?'

'Sophie,' a male voice I recognised said. 'This is Detective Pierce. How are you?'

How was I? Where to begin…

'Fine,' I said.

'We need to ask you some more questions,' the detective said. 'I'd like you to come back to the police station this afternoon. Would that be okay with you, Sophie?'

'No,' I said. 'I can't do that.'

'Why?' Detective Pierce's voice was as calm and level as usual.

'Because you're trying to frame me for crimes I didn't commit,' I said, trying to keep my tone unruffled too. 'Lisa's left me in no doubt about that.'

'Lisa?' Detective Pierce sounded genuinely puzzled. 'Ah no, I think you must have misunderstood whatever she's been saying to you.'

'No, I haven't,' I said. 'She's made it quite clear that you're going to arrest me, just like you did with my uncle.'

'That's an entirely different situation,' Detective Pierce said. 'Oliver's DNA was found on Luke's body.'

'I see. Are you sure someone didn't plant it there?' I said. 'Also, there's something not right about Lisa Denton.' I didn't care anymore, I needed to tell someone. 'She's done something to my brother Jack – she's made him more poorly again.'

There was a pause on the other end of the phone.

'You've been under a huge amount of stress recently, Sophie,' the detective said. 'And it's completely understandable that you want to find people to blame for what's happened to your family. I've worked with Lisa for nearly seven years now, and I can assure you she is a trustworthy professional who is very good at her job. There's no way she would do anything to your brother, or you, or anyone else. I think it would be a good idea for you to get some support, to maybe get in touch with a counsellor who can help you through this difficult time.'

'Goodbye, Detective Pierce,' I said, ending the call. I saved his number so I could avoid answering it the next time he rang. I didn't want anyone else to invalidate what I was saying, or to not believe me. I'd had enough of that. I could feel anger rising in me just from the short exchange with the detective.

What the fuck was I going to do now?

CHAPTER FORTY-TWO

I could trust no one at all. Zach, my friend and confidante, my dear compatriot, had disappeared off the face of the earth. I couldn't trust Oliver – even though he'd done a convincing act of not being the one who broke into my house. He was a slippery drug dealer. I definitely couldn't trust Lisa or anyone else in the police. I was one hundred per cent sure she'd done something harmful to Jack. I definitely couldn't trust religious people. Maybe Lisa had connections with my parents' old church? Perhaps that was where she'd come from, where her quarrel lay? I had no Macreavy family left – apart from a comatose brother; and I had no idea where my biological family were and they were all messed up anyway. I'd never been allowed to make friends, so had none of those. All I had was myself. But the problem was, I had no idea what to do now. My bones ached with tiredness and my stomach whined with hunger. I looked down at the beach below me, wondering if it would be easier just to throw myself over and end it all.

More memories of Sunday night came flooding back. How I'd been stumbling along in the dark, not knowing where I was going, feeling horrendously vulnerable and unsafe... just before the horror happened that I wanted to forget... But I didn't want to think about that awful time right now. I couldn't afford to, I needed to keep my head in the here and now. I had to remember I had a right to live. I had to get that strength running through my veins again.

My phone jerked into life. I stared at it. I didn't recognise the number. I didn't want to answer – but what if it was the hospital calling about Jack? I pressed the green icon.

'Hello?' I said.

'Sophie.' It was Detective Warner. 'We've just been interviewing your uncle, Oliver. He's implicated you in the murder of your brother Luke. We now have copies of all the emails you've sent each other over the last six months, we know exactly how you planned the murders, and why. I'm afraid we need to take you into custody, Sophie. If you come to the police station now of your own accord, things will be a lot easier for you...'

I ended the call, saved her number so I could always avoid it in future, and turned off my phone, my hands shaking. The black cloud above me burst and in seconds I was drenched. As if my life couldn't get any worse. It just had. Now my uncle had turned on me. He was a liar.

And what fucking emails was she talking about?

CHAPTER FORTY-THREE

A storm was raging overhead by the time I reached my front door, my waterlogged clothes all stuck to me. I turned my head away from Mr Finney's face as I fumbled for my key. He seemed to have been trying to open his window. He was shouting something, it sounded like 'I have something to tell you', but I couldn't be sure. I didn't have time for Mr Finney or anyone else right now. I needed to grab what I could, pack for the long term, and disappear. I'd never got very far with this endeavour before, no matter how many times I'd fantasised about leaving. I'd only gone for a few hours, before returning to the house again. But this time was different, I had no other choice. I needed to buy myself thinking time, go to a place the police wouldn't find me. So I couldn't stop. I had to keep going.

Minutes later I was inside, the door shut firmly behind me. Had someone been inside my house again while I was out? Did anything look different? I knew I was cracking up with paranoia but I couldn't do anything about it. It all looked the same, but who knew, maybe I was wrong.

Knowing now that there was a larger rucksack in my parents' room, I went upstairs and grabbed it from their cupboard. Oh my God, what if Lisa was outside waiting for me? What if she let herself in? She had a fucking key to my house! While I was roaming the house packing everything I thought I might need for my impending indefinite disappearance, my mind was in overdrive. I was trying to work out why Lisa would want to involve herself with my family. Why she would wish us harm. The options I came up with were:

a) The most obvious – she was exacting some revenge on behalf of Jason, because he was probably Iris's biological son and hated her and the family.

b) She was a crazy lone psycho who had randomly chosen my family to fuck up for no reason.

c) She was part of the church or had something to do with why Iris and Don left all those years ago.

d) Some other bloody reason that I hadn't thought of yet.

e) I'd got it wrong and she wasn't involved at all.

At the moment I was leaning towards a. I couldn't forget the information that Oliver had told me about Iris previously having a son of her own. For some reason it was now firmly lodged in my head that the baby was Jason Stewart. But even that didn't make sense. Okay, so he might be pissed off that she gave him into care and couldn't look after him, but he looked so happy in all his social media photos. So sorted. But as I knew so well, social media was just a big farce, a charade...

When I'd finished stuffing my charger, food, drink, clothes, torch, batteries, knife, map, toothbrush and paste, wash stuff and my keepsakes from all my siblings into the rucksack, I put it down on the kitchen table and pulled my phone out. I needed to put my mind at rest about Jason; the thought that he was Iris's biological son was ballooning in my head and I wanted to find out that he wasn't so I could carry on pursuing more sensible avenues of investigation.

I did some quick Google research into how to find

birthdates in the UK, then pulled up Ancestry.com and joined their free one-month trial. Within less than five minutes I was searching Iris's maiden name – Dunhope – and date of birth. I clicked on the *'births and baptisms'* option, and a page of different options popped up. I scrolled through them, clicking on each one. None exactly matched my mother's details. But then the fifth one I tapped on made me stop and stare. Iris Dunhope, born in Exeter. That sounded about right. Registering the birth of her daughter, Sophie Dunhope. Sophie? But that was the name Iris and Don had chosen for me when I'd come to live with them. My birth name had been Jade. And a daughter? Oliver had definitely said a son. I thought for a minute. Oliver was a drugged-up idiot who didn't know what day it was, let alone the details of a child his sister had given birth to so many years ago. It would be typical of him to get the gender wrong. He probably just guessed. But at least he'd got the most important detail right – that Iris had *had* a child.

Oh Christ. Fuck, it was all making a horrible kind of new sense... Blocks of understanding were falling into place in my brain. Just to make sure I was right, I made a note of Sophie Dunhope's date of birth; twenty-seventh of August twenty-nine years ago, then opened Facebook and searched up Lisa's profile. There was no information showing at all about her birthdate or anything else. With a growl of frustration – I wanted to be out of the house ASAP – I tapped on Jason's details and scrolled down his page. I thought I remembered seeing a photo of him and Lisa celebrating something. Where was it? Ah, there it was. I clicked on the caption under the photo of Lisa and Jason sitting in a restaurant with a cake full of sparkling candles in front of them. *'A perfect way to end my girlfriend's birthday'*, he'd written. *'Now for an early bedtime as we need to be all fresh so we can watch Man City thrash Watford in the FA Cup Final tomorrow'*. I studied the photo; they were seated by a window and the sky behind them had that summer evening duskiness to it, still light with navy-blue clouds. Looked like it could be August. I didn't know what he was talking about with the FA Cup Final, but I copied and pasted the whole sentence into Google search. It immediately came up with the year that Manchester City and Watford played against each other in the FA Cup Final. And it was played on the twenty-eighth of August that year. So Lisa's birthday was on the twenty-seventh of August. She and Sophie Dunhope were one and the same person. Lisa Denton was Iris's biological daughter. Did that make her my stepsister then? For some reason – no doubt related to this – she was trying to annihilate my whole family and frame *me* for it. Shit. A gigantic ice-cold block of fear landed in my brain and oozed throughout my system as I digested the information. I needed to get out of the house right now, and far away from this crazy woman. Iris's daughter. The fucking crazy psycho.

My head felt giddy as I picked up the rucksack and hoisted it onto my back. I turned the lights off and opened the front door, slowly at first, trying to assess if there was anyone in the front garden. Not a soul. But Mr Finney was at his window, and started banging on it as soon as he saw me. Crazy old goat. I wished he'd stop, he was drawing attention to me.

I stepped out into the torrential rain, pulling my jacket hood over my head. I peeped over the garden gate and looked up and down the road. No one was around – everyone was probably inside, sensibly sheltering from the awful weather. Lisa's car was nowhere to be seen. Good.

I walked through the gate and turned right. I was planning to walk down towards the harbour, then slowly disappear from Torquay somehow. Maybe get on a boat, or a bus. I still had some of the money that Lisa had given me, I'd hardly spent any on food. My heart began to feel lighter than it had for days with every step. Freedom was such an intoxicatingly wonderful word. I could almost smell it. It was coming; the escape from Lisa, Jason, the police, Torquay, my family, everyone and everything that had made my life toxic up till now.

I followed the curve of the road round, past the old house that had been empty for years. Then there was a movement behind me, a crack on my head followed by searing pain, and my whole world went black as I fell to the floor.

CHAPTER FORTY-FOUR

As consciousness filtered back through my brain, I realised there was no way I could open my eyes even if I wanted to because there was some sort of thick tape stuck over them. It hurt and pulled when I even flickered my eyelids. The banging pain at the back of my head was so acute I nearly passed out as I tried to assess my surroundings. I could tell I was in a car. From the motion, sensations and sounds we seemed to be going at some speed. I couldn't be sure, but I came to the conclusion that I was half bent into one of the passenger footwells at the back of the car. The sickly sweet smell of an air freshener pervading the interior made me feel nauseous. My hands and feet were bound together, and there was also tape over my mouth. I'm going to die, I realised. Probably quite soon. Whenever the driver gets to where they want to go.

I listened for clues as to who was at the wheel. It didn't take long. A song came on the radio: 'Poison' by Alice Cooper, and the driver started humming softly. It was Lisa, no doubt about that. Iris's evil offspring.

Fear was jostling pain for pride of place. Anger was rearing its head too. If I got the chance, I knew I'd kill Lisa before she finished me off. I didn't survive Iris and Don to end my days like this, I kept thinking, over and over. I'd come so close to escaping all this shit. But fear was winning. It had me in its icy grasp and I was shaking uncontrollably, horrific scenarios of what was to come playing round and round in my head.

Where the fuck was she taking me? And what would she do when we got there?

CHAPTER FORTY-FIVE

I could sense the car slowing down. Gravel crunched beneath us and we came to a slow stop. I could hear Lisa undoing her seat belt, getting out of the car, slamming the door behind her. All my nerves were on high alert, expecting her to open a back door and get me out. But then there was silence, and I heard her footsteps getting fainter as she walked away. Another door slammed, this time further away. I was left in the car, shaking, in pain, freezing, and saturated by fear. A strange thought came to me: this must be what it's like waiting to be executed...

Minutes passed, each seeming like ten hours. I don't know how long I stayed there, but the pain and terror worsened with each millisecond. I was losing my mind, I knew I was.

Then I heard the far away door open again, and footsteps crunched back.

The car door near me opened and a whoosh of cold air hit me.

'Let's get you out then, shall we?' Lisa sounded freakily calm and cheerful. 'I've got something to show you.'

She grabbed my hair and pulled me upwards. I could feel clumps of it ripping out and the biting pain made me want to scream. She ripped off the tape that was stopping me from seeing, causing fresh pain to ricochet across my eyes and face.

I looked around quickly. An old, tumbledown cottage was to our left; it looked like it hadn't been lived in for years. The windows were grimy and broken, and weeds covered the sides. Damp fields rose up all around us; we were in the middle of nowhere, away from anyone that could help. It looked like a large heath, its colours all red, green and grey – with large boulders in the distance. I had absolutely no idea where I was. I was totally disorientated. The ground around us was rough, overgrown and full of stones and pebbles. It was a desolate scene.

'If you try to struggle or make a sound, I'll kill you now,' Lisa said in a conversational way. 'It makes no difference to me if I do it now or later. Do you understand?'

I nodded, hating her with every ounce of my flesh.

She unbound my feet and hands, ripped the tape from my mouth, and marched me towards the door of the building. I was so thin and weak that my legs buckled, they ached so much, but she pulled me up roughly and pushed me forwards.

Minutes later, I was sitting on a hard chair in the dingy front room of the cottage, trying to take in my surroundings. I was surprised to see that the electricity worked out here; Lisa had obviously been making herself at home for some time. A laptop lay open on a wooden table in front of the window, a small side lamp shining next to it. Could I escape? I was wondering. Could I make a run for it and have a chance of getting away from this crazy bitch? I had no idea what – if any – weapons she had here. I was in a bad way now, in a lot of pain, and I knew she'd have no trouble catching up with me.

'Welcome to my humble abode,' Lisa said with a smile. It was the sort of grin a wolf might give its prey.

'Do you own this place?' I couldn't help asking, despite the desperate circumstances. I was just so surprised that she might.

Lisa laughed, and looked at me with loathing in her eyes.

'Yep, I do,' she said. 'Funny, isn't it? A shit pit in the middle of nowhere. But then, you have no idea about me or my life, do you? Sis?'

Sis? She'd never be any sister of mine.

But I shook my head.

'So Iris was your birth mother?' I said. Keep her talking for as long as you can, Sophie, I told myself. Do anything you have to, to survive.

My words caused a change in Lisa's demeanour. I watched as she tensed up, the sickly smile leaving her face. When she looked at me I saw dark anger in her eyes.

'Yes,' she said quietly. 'Iris, your dear adopted mother, was my real parent. But she didn't want me. She gave me up while she was still in the hospital. Never even took me home. All I ever had was one photograph of her holding me. No one even told me her name. I had to find all that out for myself.'

I sighed.

'I'm so sorry,' I said, blinking. My eyes stung from the tape being ripped away. 'But honestly, Lisa, I think you had a lucky escape. Iris and Don weren't nice parents. I'm sure you had a much nicer childhood, wherever you ended up.'

Lisa stood up from her perch on the arm of the sofa, and walked towards me, thrusting her face down near mine.

'"I'm sure you had a much nicer childhood",' she mimicked in a horrible voice. 'Are you, Sophie? Are you sure I did?' She reached out and slapped me round the face. I recoiled – an instinctive movement. 'Well that's where you're wrong, I'm afraid. But then you'd have no idea about real life, would you? This is why it annoys me so much when you start whinging and whining about how awful Iris and Don were. Yes, it sounds like they weren't perfect parents at all. They were strict and authoritarian. They didn't get it all right. But abusive? No, I don't think so. My foster parents were truly abusive, Sophie. If you'd led my life, you'd know what abuse actually is.'

I stared at her, then looked down.

'I'm so sorry,' I said. 'For whatever it is you've had to go through, Lisa.' If she was going to turn this into a competition to see who had the worst childhood, I could tell quite clearly I would be on the losing end.

'Are you?' she said, then slapped my other cheek hard. 'That's nice, thanks so much. Means a lot.'

I saw her lift a foot up and aim it at my left shin. Her hard kick sent waves of pain up and down my leg, even halfway up my spine. I had no fat on me, no layers of protection. But I must stay nice to her, I knew. If I showed any other emotion she would kill me straight away.

'Sorry,' I said. 'I don't mean to sound patronising. I am genuinely sorry. It sounds like your childhood was actually awful, worse than mine.'

'Yes it was, funnily enough,' Lisa said. As I stared at her face I wondered how I'd ever thought she was pretty. All I could see in her now was ugliness; rage, resentment, bitterness and bile. Bulging, crazy eyes, her twisted mouth. Pure hate was radiating from her. She'd spent years building up to this moment, whereas for me it was all still new, still a shock. 'After social services took me away from Iris, I was put into care with dozens of other small kids. Then I was fostered by a family, but they gave me back because they discovered they were expecting a baby of their own so they didn't need me anymore. I was a disposable character back then, can you see? A child who was rejected at will. So I lived in a children's home for three years. Do you have any idea what went on in that place?'

I shook my head.

'No, you don't do you?' Lisa said, spitting each word out. 'You little innocent. So protected from life. Well, I can tell you something; the children's home was a walk in the park compared to what happened next. I was fostered by a couple who lived in this very house. Janice and Patrick. The most evil bastards in the world. It was a long-term placement; I think the idea was to give me stability and a "forever" home. As I was continuing to be fostered and not adopted, Janice and Patrick carried on getting paid; that was their only motivation to begin with – the money. Not the desperate urge to love and bring up a child. I was nine when I arrived here, and the next eight years of my life were a living hell. In fact, hell is probably nicer than what I experienced.' There were tears in her eyes now, I could see. As she talked, she was reliving her past.

'Patrick raped me for the first time on my second night at the house,' she said. 'And continued to do that every week until I ran away when I was seventeen. Can you imagine?'

I shook my head. Jesus, that was awful.

'Janice knew, she just didn't care,' Lisa went on. 'She was a bitch of a woman, she only fostered me because she wanted a slave. When I wasn't at school, I was doing her jobs; cooking, cleaning and fucking her husband. If I protested she beat me. But she was clever, good at hiding this from the rare visits from social services. And I was too scared to say anything to them as I knew I probably wouldn't be removed from the house, and I'd have to deal with Janice and Patrick's punishments for snitching afterwards. We didn't have the internet in those days, you know, in the evenings and on weekends we were totally cut off from the outside world.'

'Where are we?' I said, my voice soft.

'Dartmoor,' Lisa said, then looked down at me sharply. Of course, I should have known. I'd gazed at enough pictures of the moorland in books. 'Don't even think about screaming or trying anything stupid. Trust me, there's no one around to hear you. I found that out myself the hard way years ago. The only vehicle that ever came near here was the school bus, and even that stopped a good ten-minute walk away. I don't think even that comes here anymore; most of the buildings round here – spread far and wide apart – are derelict now.'

I swallowed and nodded. Shit, I knew a bit about Dartmoor from my incessant reading; it was all coming back to me now. It was a vast, desolate moor covering hundreds of miles. Even if I did escape I'd probably get lost and perish while trying to find my way out. My phone was in my rucksack, wherever that was. I hadn't seen it since Lisa knocked me unconscious in Torquay. If only I could find it, I could try and ring the police. They'd have to help me now. If they could see what Lisa was doing they'd understand that she was behind all this. But how likely was it that any phone signal reached all the way out here?

'Janice and Patrick sound like monsters,' I said. I didn't want her to start thinking about my bag. Maybe if I showed her compassion it would go some way to soothing her nerves.

'Oh, they were,' Lisa said through gritted teeth. 'You don't know the half of it. And the funny thing is, Sophie.' She stopped and smiled at me. 'All the time I was here, being raped and molested by Patrick and beaten by Janice, you were living with *my* mother in Torquay. *Not* being raped, by all accounts.'

I bit my lip.

'I've worked the age difference out,' Lisa said. 'When I was twelve, you were two. And by then, you were sleeping in what should have been *my* bedroom, eating *my* meals, being looked after by *my* own mother.' Fuck, I could see she was working herself up into a frenzy; her eyes were bulging right out and she was shouting at me now.

'I'm sorry,' I whispered. 'I'm so sorry, Lisa.' There was no point in telling her that life with Iris and Don was miserable. To be fair her childhood sounded a lot worse; but mine had still been shit. She'd convinced herself that I'd exaggerated everything, that I'd whinged on about it when I should actually have been grateful for living with Iris. She'd overlooked the beatings, whippings, waterboardings, neglect, continual physical, mental and emotional taunting and berating. I knew now that nothing I said would change her mind; if I spoke at all it would just make her more mad.

'And then you have the *gall*, the utter fucking nerve,' Lisa yelled, 'to make out that your life was horrendously bad. When you were living with MY OWN MOTHER!'

She lunged forward and hit me so hard I fell off the chair. I curled into a ball as she aimed kicks at any bits of me that she could. Again and again her foot connected with my flesh – or should I say my bones, as fat was something I'd never had in abundance.

When I was bruised black and blue, when every part of me ached, and my eyes were screwed shut, and I truly believed a quick death was now the best option, I could feel her energy waning, her breathing slowing down. She stopped and I could hear her footsteps walk out of the room. A tap turned on somewhere; she must have gone to get a drink. Kicking someone to within an inch of their life was clearly thirsty work.

I couldn't move. I was done. I felt ready to die now, unbearable pain was throbbing – pulsating – through every bit of my body. But – a tiny thought came to me – you've come through so much, Sophie. Why give in to death now? Why give this psycho bitch the satisfaction of getting what she wants? All fear had now left me. I felt strangely calm – amid the agony. I didn't feel sorry for Lisa; she'd been through hell as a child, but she'd become an abuser herself. It was a classic. That was a choice, she didn't have to do that. She could have chosen to go the other way, and help people instead of destroy them. And I hated her more than anything in the world. Even more than Iris.

From my position on the dirty floor, I looked around at what I could. Dusty table and chair legs, grime under the sofa. A few wispy strands of grass growing through the broken floor here and there. I couldn't see my rucksack. Maybe she'd got rid of it? Thrown it away during our journey here? In that case it would only be a matter of time before she finished me off, and nobody would ever know. She was clever like that. And she'd be free...

I heard her footsteps getting closer again.

'Get up,' Lisa said. 'Christ, you wouldn't have survived the beatings I used to get, you pathetic little cow. Come on, stand up and sit back on that chair. I've got something to show you.'

Even though my body was ruined, aching, destroyed, I didn't want another kicking, so very slowly and painfully I made myself get up and sit back on the chair. I knew I was injured on the inside as well as the outside; blood was dripping from my nose and ears; I could see fresh gashes on my arms where she'd broken the flesh, and I was pretty sure she'd ruptured the wound in my abdomen. Something was running down my cheeks, and I touched it, wondering whether it was sweat. Nope, it was more blood. I could barely remain upright; every part of me wanted to go unconscious. But my tiny chance of surviving this meant staying awake. So I dug my nails into the palms of my hands, and willed superhuman strength to help me do just that.

'So, given my early life, you can imagine what a shock it was, four years ago, to discover that my evil foster parents had left me this house in their will,' Lisa said as she walked over to the table. Her voice had gone artificially bright again. 'Stupid, ignorant bastards. To think I would ever want anything from their abusing hands. They never seemed to understand what they were doing was a crime, that it was so wrong. And I'd never wanted to come back here, I was going to sell the place for a pittance. But then I saw the photo of you and Brianna with Iris in the background online, and I knew I had to hang on to it for a bit longer. Knew it was time to right a few wrongs, if you know what I mean.' I gazed at her through blurry vision. We're more alike than you think, Lisa, I told her silently. We've been through similar pain, and neither of us ever wanted to go back to our abusive houses again. How different life would be if we could support each other right now...

But I knew exactly what she was getting at. As soon as she'd seen me in that photo, she'd wanted revenge. She'd seen what everyone else did – a happy child with a loving mother. Made famous by people's need to live vicariously through emotional snaps on social media. Then she'd done research, looked up Iris's Facebook page, and seen all the other photos. Believed, as everyone else did, that us kids were living a charmed, wholesome, varied life with two parents who loved us unconditionally. I mean, who looks at wonderful family photos and immediately thinks that those kids must be living in hell? No one. And why would they? Iris was too clever for that. Then Lisa – perhaps understandably – developed an uncontrollable jealousy, a deep hatred of my siblings and me, falsely believing we had everything she didn't; love, a good home, wonderful parents, and opportunities. That we'd stolen this away from her, that her own biological mother was ploughing tons of affection into us, when it should have gone to her – Lisa. How wrong she'd been. But she'd never understand that. She was too hell-bent on revenge and her own style of reparation.

'Come over here for a minute.' Lisa patted the wooden chair in front of the table. 'I want to show you something on my laptop.' She grinned as I stood up. 'This is the very place I invented your boyfriend, Zach.' She watched me carefully, a sick smile getting wider on her lips.

CHAPTER FORTY-SIX

B itch, I thought, moving slowly, trying to take my attention away from my hurting body. I was angry at myself for the gut-wrenching jet of hurt that spasmed through my heart. Fuck it all, of course it was her. How had I been so stupid as to think a nice guy was actually interested in me? Jesus, Zach's kindness had meant so much, it had been the best thing that ever happened to me. I'd never felt as happy as when we were messaging back and forth, as when he was showing me understanding, empathy, a way forward for the future. But it was all a lie, an invention by this wicked cow, this murdering bitch. Another way to inflict pain on me – and this was actually worse than the physical. And to think – it had been Lisa encouraging me to lie to my parents all along. Not Zach. It had been *her* who suggested I tell them I'd shown photos of Rachel's bruises to social services, not my lovely new friend. My only friend. And he didn't even exist. The terrible news didn't surprise me for long though, not now. Nothing came as a shock now that I knew who Lisa was. A throbbing, dull acceptance rapidly fell into place.

'You were sucked straight in, weren't you?' Lisa said, a

scathing tone in her voice. 'You lapped it up, you couldn't wait for your new boyfriend to get back online so you could spout drivel to him. You loved it when "Zach" told you how pretty you are, didn't you? Silly tart. You're not pretty, you're plain and forgettable. I can't believe you trusted him. Or should I say, me. You fell for the whole thing, hook, line and sinker.'

She chuckled. Wow, another arrow of hurt. Zach had been the only person in my life to compliment my looks, and it had meant so much to me. Jesus. My eyes stung as tears leaked out. Shit, I didn't want to show Lisa any weakness. I knew it was what she wanted. I sneaked one finger up to wipe the drops away, but she saw.

'Aw, poor little Sophie,' she said, sneering. 'Have I hurt your ickle feelings?'

Lisa reached round me and tapped at the keyboard.

'I just wanted you to see my handiwork,' she said, obviously satiated by the Zach bombshell. 'I've been rather clever, even if I do say so myself.'

I trained my swollen eyes at the screen. I didn't really care about anything anymore, not after realising Zach was her sordid invention, but I knew she'd hit me again if I didn't. It was at that moment that I spied it out of the corner of my eye. My rucksack, sitting on a side table underneath the window. I couldn't have seen it from my previous position on the other chair as I'd been facing a different direction.

Making sure I didn't full-on look at it, I kept my gaze trained on the laptop screen.

'Like I said before,' Lisa was saying, 'I don't care if I have to kill you now, it doesn't make much difference to me. At least I know you'll have been punished for what you did.' Wow, I thought. Like mother, like daughter. Lisa was sounding exactly like Iris. 'But,' she went on, 'initially my plan was that you spend the rest of your life in prison. That way you'd have suffered for longer, probably for even more years than I did with Janice and Patrick. I'd have enjoyed watching you be sentenced so much, loved every minute that you spent behind bars. Do you see?'

I nodded slightly. No, I didn't see how being so cruel would make her feel any different, but hey, what did I know.

'But now you know too much about me, so you'll be the next to die,' Lisa said. She was emotionless about it, as though she was explaining who was next in to see the dentist or something. 'And to be honest, having you around is getting on my nerves. It was Jason who told me I should do something to make me feel better about my past. But I think he meant going to see a therapist. Bless him. He knows nothing about what I'm doing, I planned all this on my own. He just wouldn't understand, if I tried to tell him about it. This is my own version of therapy; making sure you feel even more pain that I did. After all, you stole my mother.' She brought up an email account. 'So when you die it's going to look like suicide. No one will care anyway. They'll think it's a sign of your guilt, that you knew the police were about to arrest you, so you took the easy way out like a coward.'

I sighed. There was no point replying to this. Lisa had clearly gone off her fucking rocker.

'So you see,' Lisa said, pointing to the words on the screen. 'What I've done is leave a very clear email trail that shows you and your uncle Oliver plotting and planning the demise of the Macreavy family. The detectives already have it, and they appear to be very interested. I think they believe every word of it.'

Ah. So that explained what the detective meant by emails between Oliver and I. But several things were still puzzling me, and I had nothing to lose by questioning her about them.

'Can I just ask something,' I said, turning a bit. 'You and Zach are the same person, I know that now. And you suggested to me that I lie to Iris and Don, tell them I'd reported them to social services, and that they would be arrested and thrown into prison.'

'Yes,' Lisa said.

'But,' I went on, 'you couldn't have known what the consequences of that would be? For all you knew, they could have just laughed at me and done nothing that evening. How did you know Don would go crazy and put us all into his car?'

Lisa laughed.

'I'd already sent him a warning letter from the "social services", saying that him and Iris would be visited the next day, and that some very serious accusations had been made against them,' she said. 'Don must have taken this seriously. Honestly, it was a gift, how it all played out. When I created Zach, and got in touch with you over Facebook, I had no idea what was going to happen. All I knew was that I was going to infiltrate your life somehow, and make amends for you lot stealing what should have been mine. But I was feeling my way through it, I had no definite outcome in mind to start with. I had no clue it would happen so quickly. It was amazing when you messaged me that evening saying Don had gone mad, and was making you all get in the car. He'd told you he wanted to get away. I thought that might be it, that he would drive you all to a new place to start a new life. If he had, I would still have found you. So in fact, when I was with Oliver that night and we saw Luke and Jack standing there by the harbour in Torquay, it was a blessing, like it was meant to be. Finally life was going my way. That's when I knew I could get to the boys. Tease them a bit before they had to go. I've been winging it most of the time, Sophie. Adapting and creating as each thing happened. You all played into my hands marvellously, to be honest.'

'Hang on,' I said, turning even more until I could see her

flushed face. 'What do you mean, when you were with Oliver that night?'

Lisa rolled her eyes.

'Haven't you worked it out yet?' she said, looking down her nose at me. 'Come on, Sophie, stop being so slow. I've been Oliver's girlfriend for the last few months. He knows me as fun-loving Crystal.'

I knew my mouth was hanging open but I didn't care. I thought I couldn't be shocked anymore, but things had taken a left-hand turn and I was really surprised by this bit of news.

'Of course,' I said slowly. 'It was you who took his bracelet and put it in my bedroom. You were masquerading as his girlfriend, and when you were at his flat you nicked the bracelet, then let yourself into my house and left it there when I'd gone for a walk to cool off after we'd had words. You were messing with my head and my sense of reality. You must have had a key cut for my place when I was still in the hospital, and you'd been given a set of my house keys.'

Lisa tossed her head back, then gave me a sly smile.

'Oh, I've been having a bit of fun with you two,' she said. 'You are both so naïve, it's laughable. I've been working on a different case at the casino by the harbour for a few months now. I've been undercover there; it was all about drug surveillance to start with. I had to be disguised as a casino worker, as we knew that area was a hotspot for large amounts of substances coming in and out of the town. We had an idea who the major players were, but we needed more hard evidence. When I got to know Oliver and realised he was related to all of you, I couldn't believe it. Since I saw the photo of you, Brianna and Iris, I've really done my homework. I found out the link pretty quickly.'

'I bet you did,' I muttered.

'I created the character of Crystal before I met Oliver,' Lisa said. 'I bought a good quality blonde wig, but when I knew he was Iris's brother I ramped up my disguise and made sure I looked cheap and nasty as I thought he'd like that sort of girl. How right I was, he fell for me straight away. I made sure my personality matched his, that we shared the same interests; mainly drugs and gambling. Your – and my – uncle is a waster, I'm sorry to say. He's nothing but a degenerate loser. So unlike my beautiful mother. But he was very helpful, without knowing it. I found out your address by going through his things. And I got him talking about his family when he was high; he told me all about how Iris had adopted you four. He didn't say anything about you being treated badly though. Just that Iris was too strict, and that she'd been the same way when they were growing up together. He told me that he sometimes met up with Luke and Jack and gave them weed to smoke, because the poor boys had nothing else to do. But he didn't say anything about you having a phone, or being on Facebook. I found that out for myself. I knew what you looked like from the photo on the news with Brianna, and so when I joined the Torquay members group and saw your profile picture, I honestly couldn't believe I'd found a way to directly message you. Another gift.'

Shit, why had I joined that group? I'd just wanted to be part of something at the time, feel like I was merging into the community – even if it was only virtually. But then, how could I have known I had a crazy stepsister stalking me out there?

As I stared at Lisa, for a fleeting moment I saw a look of Iris in her. An arrogance in the eyes, a smirk on the lips. Their face shapes had similarities, I could see that now. Lisa's eyes were brown, whereas Iris's had been blue. But for a second I saw a resemblance between them, not just in looks but in character too. I couldn't believe I'd never noticed it before. Maybe I hadn't wanted to. Maybe she'd hidden it too well. I couldn't believe I'd actually liked her the first time we'd met. What a naïve fool I'd been. But not anymore...

'So you killed Luke,' I said, trying to keep my voice level.

'Yes,' Lisa said. 'I took no pleasure in it, but I had to, you see? I didn't know Iris and Don were going to die that night.' She stopped, and I saw something – puzzlement – flit across her face. Ah, I thought. You see, you're not in control of absolutely everything, are you, Lisa? There are still things that I know that you don't...

'Like I said, initially, my plan was to get rid of the other three and have you put in prison for their murders,' Lisa said, shaking her head slightly. 'You really helped me with a motive for that, with all your moaning messages about your siblings. Then I was going to present myself to Iris when she was grieving. She would have been so comforted to have her real daughter back in her life at such a poignant moment. I know she would have been. She may not have wanted me when I was born, but she would have been very proud to see the successful police officer I've become. I'm so different from you; I'm beautiful, successful, charismatic, magnetic. Jason tells me that all the time. You're just a wishy-washy nobody, Sophie. She would have welcomed me with open arms – she'd probably have been relieved to have me instead of you in her life. And let's be honest, who else would she go on to leave her house and inheritance to, once she realised just how much she loved and missed me? Some scabby adopted kids, her drug-addict brother, or her own flesh and blood, i.e. me? I just didn't think it would all happen so quickly, and in the way it did. Once you all left the house, events kind of snowballed...'

I nodded, while thinking: what a load of crap. Firstly, Iris would never have grieved for any of us. She didn't even like us. Secondly, Iris never welcomed anyone with open arms. She was too self-absorbed and narcissistic to waste emotion on others.

Thirdly, she never cared about other people's accomplishments, unless they somehow benefitted her, like when I hugged Brianna. If she'd given her daughter away once, there was no reason she'd ever want her back again. But there was no point in disillusioning Lisa. She wouldn't believe a word I said anyway.

'But then Iris, Don and Rachel were murdered...' I said.

'Yes,' Lisa said, looking puzzled again for a second. 'I really hadn't expected that to happen. It wasn't me who did that, I don't know who did. I was putting the blame on you earlier for this, but then like I said – I do enjoy fucking with your head. I wanted you to get as worried as you did. I don't actually know what happened to Iris, Don and Rachel. Probably some wasted addict – there's enough of them about in Torquay. I'm surprised you can't remember yourself; then again you're a puny little thing and your wounds were quite bad. But like I said before, I adapted and created around that event. There was nothing I could do about Iris, I couldn't bring her back. Although I was devastated by her death. It was the end of one of my dreams – having her back in my life. But I *could* repair the wrong done to me. Jason always said I needed to find a way to let my anger go. So that's what I'm doing.'

'So you decided to focus on me,' I said.

Lisa nodded. I had to turn back towards the screen as my neck was hurting.

'Yes,' she said. 'But don't you understand why?'

I shook my head ever so slightly.

'It was you who really took my place. You even took my name. Iris called me Sophie first. It's on my birth record. It was my foster parents who started calling me by my middle name, Lisa – which then stuck. I've never been able to shake it off. But Iris called you Sophie too. It's like she replaced me with you. And all the time I was living with Janice and Patrick. I was her flesh and blood, not you. You should have been abused by those evil bastards, and I should have been with Iris.'

I took a breath in, then exhaled heavily.

'So what have you done here then?' I gestured towards the screen. I didn't want her to go hysterical with rage again. I knew another beating would kill me. Her voice was already getting louder.

'Oh yes,' Lisa said. 'As I was saying, I've been rather clever, even if I do say so myself. I'll be a detective one day if I play my cards right, I've got the skills. I've bought two domains, in yours and Oliver's names. And I've created an extensive email trail between you that goes back months. It shows how you two have been planning to kill Jack, Luke and Rachel for a long while. It's clear that you enjoy being free of the ties to them; it won't be hard for the detectives to realise that you've been planning the demise of your siblings for a while because you wanted any hint of your backstory to be wiped off the face of the earth. You wanted to be truly free, and for your cumbersome family ties to be severed forever. Obviously Rachel dying with Iris and Don was an unforeseen turn of events for me, but at least it got her out of the way.' I flinched at this, I could feel my soul having a spasm. Okay, so I may feel better without my siblings around, I may be weak when it came to loving others like that, but I'd really cared about Rachel. She was the most innocent of all of us, the least able to look after herself. She deserved to go and live with a caring family who'd have nurtured her, brought her out of herself, loved her unconditionally. She did not, in any way, deserve to be got "out of the way" – especially by this vindictive witch.

'And what was Oliver's and my motive for all this?' I said, trying to put the rising venom out of my head for now. 'In your invention?'

'Money and drugs,' Lisa said simply, as though it was

obvious. 'And the inheritance that Iris and Don left is impressive; believe me, I've checked it out. They didn't seem to spend much at all. I know your uncle well enough now to understand that he's a middle man in the drug trade, an ounce-level distributor. I take it he never told you about that?'

I shook my head. I couldn't be bothered to explain what I already knew about my uncle, I was having a hard enough time as it was without risking incurring any more wrath. It seemed easier to just let her talk.

'He's involved enough for the police to have constant surveillance on him,' Lisa went on. 'That's how I came to be Crystal working at the casino in the first place. It was a completely different case to start with. In the emails I created I made it obvious that Oliver wanted more out of life; he wanted to become a more major player in the drug world, maybe even an importer. But to do that he needed a large injection of cash, which he believed he would get if everyone died. He believed he was next to inherit the property if something were to happen to the rest of the family. It's a completely believable scenario, especially as he said he convinced Iris and Don to lend him some money years ago that he then used to increase his drug flow. In fact, as you know, my colleagues have him at the station now because of his DNA that I left on Luke and Jack – it was so easy to get stray hairs from his jacket – and because they have threatened him with everything they know about him and drugs, he's started to talk.'

'Yes, I know,' I said. A pang of hurt went through me. Oliver was lying, talking about me. I didn't think that even my drugged-up uncle would stoop so low. It hadn't taken much to make him turn, to lie to save his own self, had it? 'So where did I come into this plan for money?'

'It's obvious, isn't it?' Lisa said, leaning forwards to scroll the email on the screen upwards. 'You resented your other siblings from the moment they arrived. You wanted them out of the picture, and you needed the money from your inheritance so you could set up on your own. When I was being Zach you even told me that your life was easier before Luke, Jack and Rachel arrived. So again, we have another entirely believable scenario. In fact, the emails are with Detectives Pierce and Warner now.'

'Yes, I know,' I said.

Then why are you showing them to me? I wondered. Are you as much of a narcissist as Iris, and you just want to boast to me about how clever you are?

The sound of a ringing phone cut through the air.

'Shit.' Lisa peered at the time in the corner of the screen. 'That's probably Jason. I forgot to ring him. I'm going to have to get that or he'll worry, we always stay in contact during each day. You've been distracting me, Sophie.' She turned and disappeared.

I stared at my rucksack. It was now or never. This was my only chance. Lisa was being a bit slack for once. Mustering all my last reserves of energy, I forced myself up and out of the chair. I passed an open bag that contained a shock of blonde hair – probably the wig Lisa used when she was being 'Crystal'. Two-faced wench. I walked as quietly as I could to the rucksack, each movement causing my whole body to hurt, then went out of the room and through the partially open front door.

I heard a noise behind me. I knew it was Lisa coming to see what I was doing – perhaps she'd heard me moving around? She would overpower me if she reached me; I knew she would because my body felt broken. But I had to give this a chance. Something in me – the survival instinct – kicked into gear. I took a deep breath. Then I ran.

CHAPTER FORTY-SEVEN

I chose the direction of the clump of trees to the back right of the cottage, as I thought they would provide more cover. The ground was so stony, I stumbled as I tried to build up speed.

As adrenaline started pumping round me, the pain of my wounds and bruises receded. I didn't look back, as that would have slowed me down. I just pelted along as fast as I could, while at the same time opening my rucksack and pulling out my phone. I had to slow down a bit while I pulled up Detective Pierce's number. Thank God I'd decided to save it. I tapped on it, and held the phone to my ear as I ran. Thank fuck, it was ringing.

'Hello?' It was his voice.

'It's me, Sophie, I'm at Lisa's foster parents' house on Dartmoor,' I said quickly, panting, my words tumbling over each other. 'She says she's going to kill me. She's been trying to frame me and Oliver all this time. Please hurry. Come quickly or I'm going to die.'

'Sophie?' Detective Pierce sounded concerned. 'Slow down.

Start from the beginning. I could hardly understand a word you said. Now, you say you're on Dartmoor?'

A sound behind me made me turn. It was the front door slamming wide open. I couldn't see Lisa yet but I knew she was coming.

Something – instinct? – made me tuck my phone into the waistband of my jeans without ending the call to Detective Pierce. I knew it was a long shot, it probably wouldn't work. But it was my only chance.

Ah, I thought, glancing over my shoulder and seeing Lisa exit the house. There she is. My executioner. My self-appointed nemesis. She was holding a piece of rope and a plank of wood. I surveyed the area I'd covered. I'd only made it about two hundred metres. I hadn't even got to the first tree. I knew I was well and truly fucked.

Suddenly, my energy – my newly found adrenaline – drained away as rapidly as it had arrived. But I ignored it, dug deep into my soul, and kept going, lurching on. For a few seconds I was absolutely determined not to give up the fight. I was a survivor, I'd gone through so much. And there was no way I wanted to let this psycho get the better of me. But my best efforts were too slow. I could hear her footsteps, knew she'd nearly caught up with me. The pain and aches in my body returned tenfold. I was beaten. Broken. Done. I sunk to my knees. There was no point running. I knew this was the end, and a strange calmness washed through me. I wasn't scared, angry or anything else. I was accepting.

I was going to die now, I knew I was. My only hope was that Detective Pierce would hear what was going on, and arrest Lisa. That bitch had no right to get away with yet another murder.

CHAPTER FORTY-EIGHT

When I opened my eyes, I couldn't tell if I was alive or dead. Or in purgatory. Iris had told us a lot about that place, threatened us with it, and it felt like I was there. In limbo – between existences. I assessed the situation. It took a while, because I couldn't breathe properly; there was something very thick around my neck constricting my airways, and my thoughts were floaty and untethered. Occasionally I passed out and had to go through the whole process of realisation again each time I regained consciousness. But eventually I realised I was in a car. It seemed to be the same one as before. I was lying on the back seat, I worked out, staring at the ceiling. From the whistling coming from the front, it was Lisa driving again. The same sickly air-freshener scent hung in the air.

My hands weren't bound this time, and I brought them up to whatever was round my neck. I could feel that it was thick rope. I knew instinctively that we were driving to the site of my imminent death. I now knew Lisa was intending to hang me; probably so she could say I committed suicide.

I hoped it would be a quick process. As painless as possible. I didn't want to die – I didn't feel I deserved an end like this. It seemed almost ridiculous, given everything that I'd gone through already, to just die at the hands of Lisa at such a young age. But what could I do now? I was caught, bound and injured. Lisa was in control of my fate.

We went over a bump and the rope pressed hard against my neck. It seemed to be tied up somewhere – maybe on the handle above the window? Whenever the car moved the rope strained tighter and choked me. As the welcome blackness took me over once again, I could feel myself passing out. I hoped I would never wake up.

CHAPTER FORTY-NINE

I came to as Lisa hauled me out of the car. In my floaty, dreamy, oxygen-starved reality, I looked around and had a shock. We were at the exact place where Iris, Don and Rachel had been found stabbed to death. Where I'd also been discovered covered in deep gashes. I'd never wanted to come back here ever again. The events of that night had been too awful to consciously think about again...

'Won't be long now,' Lisa said, as though she was heaving shopping bags out of a car. 'I'll have you hooked up in no time.'

I looked up and saw what she meant. There were several trees near the edge of Meadcoombe Cliff, and the one nearest us had several very sturdy-looking high-ish branches. Perfect gallows.

I was fully in my head now; I felt separate from my body. I had no intention of doing anything that made Lisa's job of hanging me any easier.

She dumped me on the grassy verge, and tried to pull me into a sitting position, but I rolled back over. A dead weight.

I saw her open the boot of her car and pull out a stepladder.

How very practical of her to think of that. She'd thought of everything.

'Can't blame you, I suppose,' she said as she positioned it under the tree. 'Don't think I'd help anyone who was about to kill me either. Oh well, good thing you're so skinny and light. I'll have this over with in just a jiffy.'

Taking one end of the long piece of the rope that made the noose around my neck, she climbed up onto the stepladder. I looked up, watching her hook it over the branch. Then she pulled, and the pressure round my neck tightened intensely.

Just before I passed out for the final time, I saw Lisa putting all her weight into pulling her end of the rope down. I was leaving the ground. She'd done it. She was hoisting me upwards. I was travelling up into the air. I was hanging... my legs were twitching...

Blackness.

CHAPTER FIFTY

FIVE DAYS LATER...

'Oh fuck, am I still alive?' It was my voice I could hear. My eyes were opening. The inside of a hospital cubicle was swimming into focus. Machines were beeping near me. There was someone sitting on the end of my bed. Oh no, not again. Lisa?

'Hi, Sophie.' It was Detective Warner's voice. 'Very good to see you. How are you feeling?'

I blinked.

She was smiling a proper smile at me. Not a fake, polite police one. And was it my imagination or did she have tears in her eyes?

'We thought we'd lost you there for a while.' There was a crack in Detective Warner's voice. 'I'm so glad you've pulled through, Sophie. The doctors say you will make a good recovery, in time. But you've been in a bad way. You sustained several internal injuries from Lisa's attack on you – which I'm told are healing well now, as well as the awful one around your neck. I wanted to be the first one to see you, and to apologise. We got it wrong. We started to suspect that you and your uncle had something to do with the murders and attacks in your family, but it was Lisa Denton all along.'

I exhaled, a tension leaving my body. So they knew. They understood what Lisa had been up to at last. They knew what she'd done, how she'd attacked me, tried to frame me, killed my siblings. Thank God for that.

Twenty minutes later, Detective Warner had finished telling me about everything that had happened while I was in the coma. How my phone – that had somehow stayed tucked into my trousers without Lisa seeing it – had remained connected long enough for Detective Pierce to hear Lisa swearing at me, berating me, telling me she was going to have even more fun choking the life out of me than she'd had when she killed Luke, and then beating me unconscious. It must have disconnected from the call at that point, but she still hadn't found it on me. She was too busy dragging me towards the car, making a noose and slipping it round my neck. Loading me into her vehicle once more.

So Detective Pierce, Detective Warner and their colleagues had had time to trace the pings of my phone to Dartmoor, then follow them as Lisa dumped me back in her car and drove me towards Meadcoombe Cliff. A whole squad of firearms officers and paramedics were sent on ahead once Detective Pierce had seen where Lisa had stopped. They arrived literally seconds after I'd passed out, hanging from the tree branch. Lisa had been arrested as she slammed the car boot down, and she was taken to the cells while I was taken to intensive care.

Once Lisa's connection to Iris was discovered, she confessed to everything. Seemed proud of it, in fact, Detective Warner said. Boasted about how she'd told Oliver she was going back to the casino on Sunday night, after she, my uncle and brothers had smoked drugs together, but in fact had lured Luke and Jack away with hints that sex and more drugs were to come. She'd flattered them, she said. Made them feel like real men for once. She'd killed Luke pretty soon as he was causing her trouble – he wasn't being quiet or compliant – then dumped him on Compington Mount, to further the mystery of what was happening to my family. Taken my father's phone with her, to cause confusion. But she'd kept Jack tied up in her cottage for a couple of days longer, had toyed with him like the abuser she was. Then she'd tried to kill him too, dumped his body in the same place as Luke's, when her colleagues had finished their forensic examination of the area. Chucked his broken spectacles next to a tree. She'd previously planted Oliver's hairs all over both boys so his DNA would be found on them. Every now and again had used my father's phone to give everyone false hope, and confuse the situation. Had even answered when I'd called it that time, breathed heavily down it, to make me think Jack was okay...

She'd admitted to stalking me online and in person, making up the character Zach and using him to gain my trust, while also extracting information from me. She'd explained how she'd recognised her birth mother Iris in the viral photo of me and Brianna, how seeing us like that had incensed her. She'd used Zach to influence my behaviour, realising how vulnerable and malleable I was at that time, before the murders. She'd wanted to stir things up, make the 'shit hit the fan' in my house – her words apparently, which is why she – or Zach – had told me to lie to Iris and Don about reporting them to the social services in the first place. She'd had no idea things would develop so quickly and dramatically that very night, but she was pleased they had. She was still denying having anything to do with the murders of my mother, father and sister, but Detective Warner said no one believed her, and that a judge and jury wouldn't either. She'd spied on me, followed me around – which is how she knew I'd gone to see my uncle recently, when I lied to her and said it had been a few months since I'd last seen him. She'd played mind games with me, made up phone calls to other police officers when she knew I could hear what she was saying. Bugged the phone she gave me so she'd always know where I was and what I was doing. Had some fun with me and Oliver, making us suspect each other – like when she dropped his bracelet in my bedroom. She had the skills that would make her a good detective. Instead, they'd made her a criminal. Shame, what a waste.

Lisa had abused her position as an undercover officer at the casino to befriend my uncle, Oliver. Originally stationed there for surveillance on the drug trafficking that was known to take place near the harbour, she couldn't believe her luck when my uncle walked in one day. Quickly adjusting her appearance over the next few days for maximum appeal – her hot pants getting ever shorter and tighter, she lured him in and they were soon an item. She combined her role as undercover officer with murderous stalker, by delighting in finding out just what a degenerate, drug-dealing criminal my uncle actually was. Through him, she found out that he had direct access to my brothers, and that he was giving them drugs behind my parents' backs. This was great news to her, as she knew she would one day get to meet my siblings and I, one way or another. When he was arrested, and the trail of Lisa's fake emails were shown to him – that at the time detectives believed to be real – my stupid, weak uncle capitulated, and decided to admit to the crime and strike a deal with police, by agreeing to testify against me. He knew he was so deep in shit by that stage – not only did he have the murders hanging over him but also multiple drug charges – that he did a quick calculation and determined that lying was his best way forward. Even if it would have meant I'd be charged with something I didn't do. I'll never forgive him for that. Never.

Although my uncle had now been cleared of any involvement in the murders of my family members – the detective said – with Lisa having admitted to setting up the fake domains in our names, and planting his DNA on my brothers, he was still being held in custody. This was because coincidentally, along with faking the evidence against him, Lisa had also provided the police with actual real evidence of his wide-reaching drug activities. They'd found his 'special' drug box packed with heroin in Lisa's old cottage – not her usual address apparently, she usually lived with Jason in a smart apartment in Torquay. But that was just the tip of the iceberg with his drug-trafficking activities, apparently. He was – at the very least – a medium player in Torquay's drug trade. Detective Warner said he was being charged and would appear in court quite soon.

She'd admitted to going to the hospital to try and finish Jack off, once the doctors told her he'd started to talk. Brought some animal poison on her way there, that had the dangerous chemical – Compound 1080 – in it. She'd googled the fastest-working odourless poison the night before, just in case, knew exactly where to get it the next day. Apparently she'd smuggled it into the hospital in a plastic syringe, and was planning to squirt the whole lot into my poor brother's mouth. But she'd been disturbed after the first drop had gone in – Jack was resisting as much as he could, as he could move his head a bit by then – so she'd had to stop, as then the nurse came in to take his blood pressure. Also, Lisa said she'd wanted to leave before I arrived – she suspected that I'd been given the news that my brother had started talking too. One of the doctors who'd treated my brother after Lisa's efforts to kill him came to see me when I was recovering in hospital, before I'd had my long chat with the detective.

'It's very lucky that Jack had only had one drop of

Compound 1080,' he'd said to me, his face tired and serious. 'Any more, and he'd most certainly be dead.'

As it was, the doctor explained my brother had gone into a coma that had lasted three days – then opened his eyes once again.

'But due to the interference of the chemical with his respiration and circulation systems,' the doctor said, 'I'm afraid he would most likely be brain-damaged for the rest of his life. I'm so sorry to tell you this, Sophie.'

My poor brother, I'd thought, my heart aching. *He'll be in special care for the rest of his life.*

Detective Warner said that our next-door neighbour, Mr Finney, had come to the station and given a statement about Iris and Don while I was unconscious. Apparently he'd been worried about me, after he found out I was back in hospital. The newspapers had had a field day reporting on everything, and coverage had even reached the national press. He'd explained that he was a former member of my parents' church, and he felt he finally had the courage to divulge what had happened all those years ago – the schism that had caused my parents to leave it so abruptly. He wanted to share the information in case it helped the police catch whoever was doing this to me and my family – at the time he came in, Lisa's arrest wasn't public knowledge – the papers had just detailed the fact that an unnamed woman had tried to hang me, and was now in custody. Apparently, all those years ago, Iris had been suspected of defrauding the parish. At the time, she was helping the priest by being his treasurer; responsible for looking after the donations and collection money given by parishioners. She was in charge of the bookkeeping too, and all had seemed well with the accounts for years. But then when an external Catholic auditor came to check up on things, and ran his eye over Iris's accounting records, he found rather gaping inconsistencies with what money should be there and what actually was. Mr Finney – who was a lay minister at the time – said he witnessed a rather ugly scene one day. The local priest, Father Sheehan, had called Iris and Don to his study, as well as his two ministers and other trusted lay people including Hattie and the others from Don's list, to try to get to the bottom of where all the parish money had gone. The church needed a new roof at that point, and there should have been enough to pay for it, but in actuality it wasn't there. Mr Finney said that the priest was approaching the matter delicately – as everyone there still believed Iris was far too much of an upstanding citizen to be involved with anything so heinous, and that there must be some mistake. But as soon as she was even mildly questioned about the discrepancies in the accounts, Iris had lost her temper and accused Father Sheehan of bullying. 'After everything I've done for you,' she'd apparently shouted. 'You accuse me of being a thief.' At which point she and Don had stormed out.

Yep, I thought, as I listened to the detective tell the story. That sounds like Iris. Causing a problem, then unable to take responsibility for it. As her guilt in the matter was only suspected, but not proved, it had never been taken any further – and the church members had not spoken publicly about it – it left her wider public reputation untarnished. But those involved had formed a deep distrust of the Macreavy name from then on, which is probably why they'd refused to speak to me on the phone. Mr Finney had left the church himself at a later date, disliking the unfriendly cliques he found to be there. And all this time, I'd thought something really serious and awful had happened to make my parents leave the church. But in actual fact, the simple truth was that Iris had fucked up, and was worried about the truth coming out and ruining her well thought of reputation. She just couldn't take responsibility and say sorry, so instead she and Don started a weird religion at home, taking on the roles of priests – which in their eyes, gave them even more power over us. Bastards. I had an inward chuckle as I digested the hypocrisy shown in my mother's actions. Outwardly so perfect, yet in reality thieving church funds. Maybe none of us on this earth are quite as flawless as we'd like to be?

Lisa was a psychopathic narcissist, Detective Warner said. That's what the psychiatrist she'd seen had diagnosed her as, following her arrest. Which made complete sense to me. An extraordinarily dangerous woman. Formed partly from Iris's defective, sadistic genetics, and partly from her horrendous childhood and teenage experiences. She'd suffered a great deal, but now she'd chosen to inflict even worse pain on others. They had enough physical evidence, plus her confession, to put her away for life, Detective Warner said. She was being charged with the murders of Iris, Don, Rachel and Luke, and the attempted murders of Jack and I. Apparently she was continuously ranting about these charges, trying to say they weren't accurate, that they were flawed, but no one was taking her mumblings seriously. She'd proven to be the murderer; the scorned, abandoned daughter with an axe to grind, and that was that.

I watched as the detective reached into her bag, pulling out a newspaper. She laid it on the bed in front of me.

Disgraced Police Officer Charged with Multiple Murders of Her Own Estranged Family, I read. *Lisa Denton, formerly a family liaison officer with Devon and Cornwall Police, has been charged with the slaying of her biological mother, Iris Macreavy, as well as the murders of Don Macreavy, Rachel Macreavy, Luke Macreavy, and the attempted murders of Jack Macreavy and Sophie Macreavy. Detectives were alerted to Denton's last act of senseless violence by a phone call made by Sophie, just moments before the nineteen-year-old was beaten unconscious by Denton.*

Police were able to trace the location of the phone, and arrived at Meadcoombe Cliff just as Denton was attempting to hang Sophie – the adopted daughter of Iris and Don Macreavy – from a tree. This heinous act took place on the exact spot that Denton is believed to have murdered her own mother – and two others – the week before. Detectives say that Denton has confessed to killing Luke Macreavy, and the attempted murders of Jack and Sophie Macreavy. They say they believe it is just a matter of time before she confesses to the three murders of Iris, Don and Rachel. Jack and Sophie remain in hospital, their conditions are believed to be critical but stable... It was strange, I thought – how quickly newspapers changed the angle of their stories. One minute they were saying I was a suspect in the murders, but now I'm a victim and Lisa is the evil witch. The power the media has over people's thoughts and beliefs is crazy...

'So don't you worry about Lisa,' Detective Warner was saying. 'I doubt she'll ever get out of prison once she's found guilty. You can lead the rest of your life in peace, love, without having to worry about her again.'

I smiled, and looked at the rays of the sun shining through the hospital window.

Something about her words had given me an idea...

CHAPTER FIFTY-ONE

T he coach rolled along the country lanes away from Torquay, following curve after curve in the long winding road. I rested my head against the window, enjoying the bumpy sensation. I was loving seeing sights I'd never clapped eyes on before. Here was a waterfall, there was a village called Ipplepen. It was all new, all fresh and unknown to me, and I was enjoying every minute.

I let the awfulness of my years with Iris and Don, and the trauma of psycho Lisa Denton – and everything that had happened in between – start falling away with each mile I travelled. There was a lightness in my chest, I noticed, a fizziness in my stomach. This time, I'd actually managed to make a fresh start. I'd got away. I was actually on the move. And my reputation was intact – everyone had been so kind – I had money in my pocket from the police fund, new clothes, and the rest of my life in front of me.

I'd explained my idea to nice Detective Warner – about how I wanted to get out of Torquay and see the world a bit. Live somewhere else for a while, travel, and have a fresh start. She'd helped me organise everything, made sure I bought the right coach ticket, helped me book several months' worth of accommodation across the UK and Europe. I felt a wonderful tingle rush through me, as I realised I'd actually be able to see the Eiffel Tower soon, rather than just stare at photos of it in a book. I'd be able to touch the ancient Greek stones of the Colosseum, gaze at Renaissance art in Florence. Walk through the Brandenburg Gate, gaze at the Seine, there was so much to do. I was actually going to live life, rather than read about other people doing so. It was something I'd dreamt about at home with Iris and Don, but that I never thought would come true. And now it was. And it was a rush, a dizzy wonderfulness, to realise this.

Which was strange, all things considered. That I'd managed to get away, I mean. Because, after all, there was a bit more to the story than anyone else knew. And they would never know the whole truth, I would make sure of that.

The thing is, I now realised that Lisa had done me a favour by getting rid of Luke and Rachel. And Jack... well. He'd be in a special home for the rest of his life, fully funded by the government. There was no need to worry about him. The doctors said he would be brain-damaged for the rest of his life; thanks to Lisa's dirty work. I didn't need to hang around and spoon-feed him, there would be plenty of paid doctors and nurses around him for that. He'd probably never even recognise me again. I was a free agent now. No Iris, Don, Rachel, Luke or Jack to hold me back.

And the funny thing is, that evil bitch Lisa ended up taking the rap for something I was responsible for, rather than the other way around as she was intending. You see, I can remember exactly what happened after I got out of the car, about what took place, and how I ended up sitting next to my dead sister covered in stab wounds. That Sunday night, when Don had gone mad and made everyone get in the car, an incident took place that was entirely unanticipated. Completely unplanned and unforeseen. After Luke and Jack had disappeared – I now know they went with Oliver and Lisa (who was pretending to be Crystal) – I'd decided to make a run for it. I've always wanted to get away from Torquay. That night was my first chance to put my plan into action. But at that time I had no money at all. I was technically still under the iron control of Iris and Don. I didn't think like I do now. I had no awareness of the world. I was inexperienced, I didn't know what the hell I was doing.

So I just set off walking into the night, in a direction that I guessed was away from the town. That was my only plan; to keep going until I got somewhere new. Then I'd figure out what to do when I arrived. I walked off into the horrible black night, with no phone, no funds, no map, nothing. On and on I'd gone, noticing that the ground level was gradually getting higher. I'd walked for what seemed like hours, through residential streets, up main roads, down side roads, through torrential downpours.

Then something unexpected happened. I'd found myself in a more open space. I could hear the splashing and heaving of waves. I could see by the dim light of the moon that I was near the sea. The pale rays were coagulating on the waves like clotting blood. From the biting, harsh wind, and from the distance down to the sea, I knew I was somewhere high up and exposed. Probably near the edge of a cliff.

Then I saw the car's headlights. I didn't want to see any other humans on my journey; I was trying to escape from my life and I didn't want anyone to get in the way. But I had to pass the car, there was no other way forward and I didn't want to go back. As I got closer, I knew, just knew it was Dad's car. I recognised the number plate and the shape. I mean, what are the statistical chances? I escape from my parents, then I run into them again. Maybe I could run past without them seeing me...

'Sophie!' It was Iris's harsh voice. She'd spotted me. Like the well-trained robot I was, I turned towards the car as though a magnetic force was pulling me. Iris opened her door and the car light came on. That's when I saw them. The bodies of Rachel and Don. They were covered in blood, and very still. Rachel's eyes were open but her stare was dead, I knew instantly that she was gone. And Don's mutilated body was lifeless, no breathing, no noise. It was obvious that he was deceased too. I didn't have to touch them to know this; just looking at them was enough; no one could have survived the injuries Iris had inflicted on them. I didn't care much about Don but the evil bitch had killed my little sister. She'd ended poor, defenceless Rachel's life. It's too horrific, the shock of that discovery will never leave me. What the fuck gave her the right to behave like that and play God? Red-hot anger swelled through me, pushing any horror and fear away that I felt. I looked down and saw that Iris still had a knife in her hand.

'Come closer, Sophie,' Iris said. She reached her hand out. 'Can't you see, this is the only way? We're finished here on the earth now, us Macreavys. God is waiting for us to come to heaven. It won't take a minute, I promise...'

A whole film reel of thoughts flashed through my mind in an instant. I had another choice to make. I could either let Iris kill me, or I could kill her. There would be no other way, no chance one of us could escape. If the first option happened I'd be dead. If the second option happened, I'd be alive and free. No contest, especially not after what this bitch had put me through all these years. I lunged forward, grabbed the knife – she wasn't expecting me to so she didn't resist. With all my might I plunged it deep into my mother's chest. God, it felt good to hurt her for once. All the years of repressed fury and rage were welling up fast, and I withdrew the knife, then plunged it into her body over and over again, until she was limp, still and covered with blood that oozed from her and dripped to the ground. Then I dragged her back to the front passenger seat, an almost superhuman strength – adrenaline – having taken me over. As I was nearly finished and was stuffing her legs into the footwell, I heard a car coming. Saw its lights. Without a second thought, I jumped into the back of the SUV next to my dead sister, slashed myself a few times for good measure – some quite deep cuts – then shut my eyes. As the car's headlamps illuminated the bloodbath inside the car, I heard it slow down and stop. Two doors opened. Footsteps. A gasp and a scream.

'My God,' a man's voice said. He was talking quickly and it sounded like he was breathing very fast. 'Look at what's happened here. Jesus, it's a massacre. Quick, phone the police.'

'Okay, but we need to get back in our car and lock the doors,' a woman's voice said. She was crying now. 'I can't believe this, I've never seen anything so horrific. Those poor people.' Her voice stopped for a minute. When it started again, there was a fearful tone to it. 'The thing is, we don't know if someone dangerous is still out here.'

As I listened to their car doors slam shut, I realised that I was the most dangerous person out there right at that moment. I'd just killed my own mother. But I wasn't about to harm them. They hadn't done me any wrong. It felt good to be powerful for once.

Soon, sirens were screaming through the night air. I pretended to be flitting in and out of consciousness as the paramedics lifted me out of the car and onto a stretcher.

Like I've admitted before, I sometimes have trouble telling the truth, even to myself. I buried what happened in that car for days afterwards; when the detectives told me Rachel was dead it was even a shock because I'd blanked it out. But from that moment on, bits – details – of that incident came back to me in dribs and drabs; sometimes when I was awake, at others during my dreams. In my sleep I often saw Rachel looking at me, shaking her head. I know why. It's because she thinks I should have been more honest from the start. She's not annoyed that I defended myself against Iris, she understands that I had to do that. But she's disappointed in me, she wants me to be a better, more authentic, straightforward person. But I don't know if I can do that; years of Iris and Don's 'nurture' have affected me, and I am who I am.

So I've known – fully and consciously – for a few days now, that we didn't need to look for who murdered Don, Iris and Rachel. It was Iris who slayed my father and sister. And it was me who ended her life. But I couldn't tell anyone that, oh no. I had to keep pretending we were just looking for one frenzied murderer who was after my whole family. Because the police wouldn't have understood if I'd tried to tell them. It would have complicated things – I mean look at the shitshow that happened when they found out I hadn't even been honest about nicking Don's old phone.

But the good thing is, I can look at what I did and be truthful with *myself* now. When the detectives first came to see me in hospital I was in denial, I was traumatised; so much had happened in a short space of time. My whole life had changed in a heartbeat. At that point, I'd yet to understand that transformation I'd undergone, from a controlled, meek wallflower to a feisty woman who wasn't afraid to kill in self-defence. And that's exactly what it was that night: self-defence. It was Iris or me who was going to die, and I chose Iris. I'd reckoned that she'd had her chance to live life, and now it was my turn. But no police officer, detective, lawyer or judge would ever understand that. Which is why that particular snippet of information will stay firmly in my head forever and never see the light of day.

It might sound harsh to say that I'm relieved my siblings are no longer around me; being either dead or brain-damaged. Don't get me wrong, I never wanted them killed or anything. I would never have harmed them. I cared about them, in a watered-down kind of way. However, if truth be known, I also *did* resent them for having arrived and making my life harder. Lisa was right about that. Iris turned into a turbo bitch the moment they were adopted. Also, I was tired – exhausted – worn out, by the tedious, brutal life we all lived. I simply wouldn't have been able to go forward in life if my sister and brothers were still around me. I would never have been able to fully shake the trauma and memories, the residual attachments we would have had. I care about myself now. No one else does, so I have to. I have to come first in my life. So in actual fact, psycho Lisa has done me a good turn. I couldn't have planned it better myself.

On the way to the coach station, I stopped and read the front page of *The Record* outside a newsagent. *'Murderous Cop to be Charged with Assassination of Birth Family'*, the headline said. Which wasn't strictly accurate – as my siblings and I weren't her blood relations, but hey. I skimmed the article, and it made me smile how they'd consulted a learned psychologist, Dr Volkov, for his take on the whole thing. He'd talked about abandonment issues, psychopathy, how the ideal image of happy families constantly portrayed in the media gives more vulnerable members of society an unrealistic benchmark to live up to. Actually Dr Volkov, I'd thought, I can give you a shorter explanation: Iris was a bitch, and her daughter was one too. Is it nature or nurture? Both. Nature with Lisa, nurture with me. Because let's face it, I'm a bit of a bitch too, I guess. Not entirely – some of me is nice, but it's there – otherwise I wouldn't be relishing my freedom from my siblings, would I? I wouldn't have killed my mother – albeit in self-defence. With me it was nurture, Iris damaged me for so many years. But then again, maybe I would have felt like this anyway. Who knows?

So now the good thing is that I can shake away all family

ties. I guess I have duality in me too. I'm like Lisa and Iris; a mixture of dark and light, good and bad; and I'm not sure about the percentages or quantities of each. And I don't actually care, because it doesn't matter now. I'm free. And like I said before, I am who I am, and I've accepted that now. And I'll keep my secret about what I did to Iris to myself until I go to my grave.

So thank you, Lisa Denton, for taking the rap for Iris's murder, and for breaking the familial chains that were holding me back. You've done me a huge favour. I guess we're more alike than I thought. Sis.

THE END

A NOTE FROM THE PUBLISHER

Thank you for reading this book. If you enjoyed it please do consider leaving a review on Amazon to help others find it too.

We hate typos. All of our books have been rigorously edited and proofread, but sometimes mistakes do slip through. If you have spotted a typo, please do let us know and we can get it amended within hours.

info@bloodhoundbooks.com

Printed in Great Britain
by Amazon